DRAGON ROGUE

Dragon Rogue
A Dragon Island Book
Jodi Kendrick

SoulGate Publishing

Dragon Island

Dragon Heat
Dragon Rogue
Dragon Blood

EveL Worlds : FUCN'A

Tough Nut
Diamond in the Ruff
Honeyed Nut
Gorilla in the Hiss
FUCN'A Collection One
Pedigree Collection

Global Paranormal Security Agency

Awakened
Surfacing
Polestar
Aquatic Investigations
Prowler

Enchanted Ardor

Wish

Finely Aged

Dragon Steel

The Kindred Chronicles

Healer
Mercenary

The Nightshade Guild

Destined Time
Trial by Blood

The Soaring Dragon Chronicles

Return Flight
Changeling

Aeleftheria Nisi

A hidden archipelago in the Bermuda Triangle, Aeleftheria Nisi is a thriving community of female dragon shifters and a few humans that live independently of any males.

In fact, they're not welcome.

Centuries ago, the Queen and her council decided to break away from the domineering rule of the male dragons to govern themselves.

Some of the male dragon tribes are determined to bring the females back under their control.

The females will fight to the death to ensure their sovereignty.

Chapter 1

Black River

Dragonsdammit, Marli, you've only been gone a few days and your mission is already fucked.

Aeleftherian Guardian Marli Fleetwing adjusted the angle of her wings, expanding the arc of her search spiral as the moon descended and the sky lightened, outside of the town of Black River. The human world would soon awaken.

The queen tasked you with ensuring Aeleftheria's safety.

Simple.

Find the mountain lair, make sure your pregnant best friend's new mate doesn't betray us, and then get everyone home safely.

Gliding over the darkened treetops, Marli scanned the shadowy ground. The muscles in her back ached from hours of flight, searching for Kymri Steelscale and Kymri's partner, Jori Mountainside.

Marli searched the landscape between the town, Heidi Brandt's homestead, and the nearby shifter refugee camp, in the hopes she'd spot them on foot, while Odson Blackridge searched much further out, toward the ocean.

They're just not here.

Marli shunted away terrible thoughts of what could have happened. Images of Kymri's inert body—dragon form or human form—invaded her mind, ratcheting up her anxiety.

She's likely still in her human form since Jori can't shift and her pregnancy makes it harder for her to hold her dragon form, anyway.

She wouldn't abandon him.

Kymri, why'd you have to go and bond with him, *of all people?*

Marli's claws skimmed the tops of several trees, startling her nervous system into flapping her wings, pushing herself higher into the night sky.

Where did those male dragon assholes go?

Stenlen Flintail, leader of the enemy males who were hunting her Aeleftherian sisters, had shown up outside of the club in Black River looking for Marli's friend, Odson Blackridge. He'd dropped the bomb that Jori was the heir of Aeleftheria's greatest enemy, King Kargassa of the mountain tribe.

If I see that asshole again, I'm going to sink my claws into him and rip him apart.

Marli had stopped Odson from doing it because they'd been in the middle of Black River. She guessed Stenlen had engineered that as part of the encounter. Neutral ground.

She snarled as fatigue made it harder to resist gravity dragging at her.

A shadow passed in front of the moon, drawing her attention.

Odson circled around, having returned from his search efforts further toward the coast.

He huffed as he glided past her position.

Nothing.

Fuck.

Her mission had been to ensure that Jori wasn't a threat to Aeleftheria.

Instead, Stenlen's men had somehow abducted Kymri and Jori while he had occupied Marli and Odson's attention.

Someone had also tampered with the security cameras around the club, rendering them useless in determining what had happened.

So, now Jori is the king's heir? He and Kymri are missing, and I still don't fucking know where the mountain lair is.

The queen was counting on me, and I put Aeleftheria at even more risk.

Heart heavy, back aching and wings tired, Marli followed Odson back to the Brandt family home, overlooking Black River.

Dragon Mountain

———◦·╼◦╾·◦———

Stenlen Flintail stared at his former wingmen through the cell doors of their dungeon prison.

Merwin growled, "We're not taking the fucking loyalty oath, Sten, so you can just piss off and leave us alone if you're not here to release us."

Sten shrugged, turning his back on the two males. He wasn't going to waste his time. There were too many other issues popping up all over the mountain that he had to deal with.

"Asshole," Clive called after him.

Stepping into the stone passage, Sten closed the antechamber door.

"Fucking traitor."

Sten spun at the growl, facing the male that uttered the words. Gritting his teeth, his eyes narrowed on Craig, one of the former king's deputies.

Former king. King Kargassa of the mountain tribe, who had ruled for centuries.

Sten swallowed.

My fault.

"What's going to happen to Clive and Merwin?"

"That's up to the new king." Sten shrugged.

"Usurper," Craig spat.

Sten sauntered toward Craig, heart pounding, fingers curling into fists. "You were there. You saw what happened."

Craig's features tightened.

"The entire tribe witnessed Kargassa name Mountainside as his heir. No one can deny that. If Kargassa couldn't have predicted what happened next, how could any of the rest of us?"

"Mountainside murdered him. Kargassa's blood is on you."

Yes, it is.

He swallowed the rising guilt.

"And for what? A couple of Aeleftherian bitches?" Craig pressed.

Sten stepped into Craig's personal space. "Is that who we are? A tribe of males that murder defenseless females on a whim?"

"He was our *king*."

"He was." Sten nodded.

And I will bear the responsibility of his death for the rest of my life.

My king, my mentor.

"Is there anything else you'd like to address?" Sten's gaze flicked up and down at the deputy, then levelled on his eyes. "You took the oath. If you've changed your mind, you know your options."

Craig's lips compressed as he jerked his head. "No, sir."

"Good. Eamerson handles complaints. I just enforce the rules." He turned to go.

"Do you?" Craig sneered.

Sten hesitated, glaring at the other male over his shoulder. He straightened, fists balled even tighter. "You know I always have."

Until I was forced up to a line that I wouldn't cross...

He continued on, leaving Craig at his post.

It wasn't the first confrontation since Kargassa's unexpected death... nor would it be the last.

Chapter 2

Black River

Brandt Homestead

Marli Fleetwing stifled a yawn, rubbed her hands over her face, then through her tangled hair.

Defeated, sun up, she and Odson had returned to the Brandt homestead to exchange updates.

She slouched, forcing a smile as Heidi Brandt set a steaming cup of coffee on the table before her. "You are my new favorite hero, Heidi." She reached for the cup, wrapping her fingers, with their metallic purple nails, around the cup.

"Coffee. Domestic heroism at its best." Heidi laughed.

"Don't knock it. It's more powerful than you may realize," Odson Blackridge grunted with a nod as Heidi handed him a cup before taking her seat at the solid harvest table that filled the dining room.

Heidi's house was quiet now after the chaos of the last few days, in the search for Kymri and Jori.

"I'm going to have to report what's happened soon. I can't hold off much longer." Marli's eyelids threatened to slam shut. She stared at the steam rising from her cup as her thoughts turned to her island home. "As soon as we find Kymri, I'm taking her back to Aeleftheria, then I'm going home to my cozy bed. For a solid week."

"I still can't believe Clive and Merwin abducted them with no hint or trail. There's no way Stenlen didn't organize everything for them before our little rendezvous in the street; I seriously doubt those knuckleheads are capable of it on their own."

Marli snorted. She stared at her wavering reflection in her cup as she considered the three male dragon shifters that had attacked her island home, then abducted Kymri and Jori. "Any word from your agency friend?" She asked Odson.

"Carson? He's working on a couple of cases right now, but his people are still scouring the satellite data for this area—well, as much as possible anyway. Black River's magical atmosphere isn't as powerful as Aeleftheria's, but it's strong enough to be a problem for the satellites."

"Blaine is sure a vehicle was used to disrupt the scent trail. Neither he, nor any of my other boys, picked up the dragon scents beyond the alley behind the club where they were last seen." Heidi sipped her coffee. Her grown sons were bear shifters and dedicated Black River guardians, like she and her husband were. "You should stop by the refugee camp. Maybe they know something. With the camp so close, all kinds of shifters pass through there all the time. I'm willing to bet that those males stopped there on their way to Black River."

"Nah, I don't want to drag the camp into this. They have their own problems. Besides, the whole point of its existence is to avoid tribal politics."

Heidi lifted a brow, staring back at the old dragon shifter. "No one is avoiding dragon politics right now, Odson. It's spilled into Black River."

"I should have taken Stenlen out when I had the chance."

"I'm glad Marli stopped you before you could. You'd have destroyed the town."

"We couldn't have known they were going to abduct Jori and Kymri. We believed their focus was on taking control of Aeleftheria." Marli rubbed her hands over her face again. "I can't believe Jori is their king's heir. What a freaking mess."

"Heir?" Heidi's other brow raised as her gaze shot back to Odson. "You didn't mention that important bit of information."

His expression turned haunted.

"That's what Stenlen said when he delayed us outside of Blaine's club. As soon as I find their lair, I'm going to rip that bastard apart."

"Not if I get to him first." Marli's hands tightened on her mug.

"You know we'll help with anything you need, so long as the ripping happens outside of Black River," Heidi said. "Just call us."

Odson nodded. "Thank you, Heidi. You and your family have already done enough for us—for everyone, really. I'm going home to shower and make a few more calls."

"I'll go with you, then head out on another search after sunset." Marli gulped down the rest of her coffee.

As they rose from their seats, their phones buzzed.

Marli pulled her cell from her pocket.

Odson snatched his phone from the table, breath hissing through his teeth as he read the screen.

Marli's heart tripped as she read the message from Jori aloud. "The king is dead. Elora is alive. Bring Jonathan to the mountain." The coordinates followed in the next message.

"What the hell happened?" Heidi shot to her feet, looking from Odson to Marli. "Elora's alive? After all this time? That's—that's good. I'm so glad she's reunited with her son," she breathed, blinking away the tears that suddenly welled in her eyes.

"That's all it says, but I'm going to find out what's going on." Marli shoved her phone into her pocket.

Odson growled, pulling the keys to his Mustang Shelby from his jeans. "*We*. My sister is alive. *We're* going to find out. Let's go."

Relief that they were all alive warred with the gut churning knowledge that she was about to go into her enemy's domain with little more information than that.

Every Aeleftherian's worst nightmare.

Chapter 3

Heart pounding, Marli leaned as the small plane eased around the mountain peak.

Through the windshield, the mountain peaks were phantoms in the mist, and the forest below was a thick carpet in various hues of green shot with silvered rivers, creeks and waterfalls.

She wasn't anxious because she was a dragon forced into a Cessna—she'd become acclimated to human air transportation over the years. As an Aeleftherian guardian heading for the maw of her long-time enemy's lair, she was anxious to unleash her claws and get scaly.

The one thing that her colony had fought tooth and claw to avoid was being dragged back into this male-controlled mountain.

And she was going willingly. Mostly.

Jonathan Mountainside, the human male that Jori had known as his father, piloted the small plane, aligning it with the open cavern containing the runway, embedded in the mountain's side.

Returning her gaze to the open flight strip, her pulse calmed seeing that Kymri waited for them. The bunched muscles in her shoulders relaxed and she drew a deep breath, easing it out through her nose. It had occurred to her since they'd read the message from Jori that they could be flying straight into a trap. Despite Odson's agreement, neither of them were deterred.

Jonathan gasped as the figures waiting for them came into focus for his human eyes a moment later.

His wife stood next to Kymri.

He blinked away gathering tears as he brought the plane into the cavern. Elora had been missing for two decades.

As soon as the plane stopped, he cut the engine, shut everything down, and was shoving the door open before either Marli or Odson could rise from their seats.

Exchanging glances, they followed him out.

Marli's gaze swept the massive cavern that served as an airstrip, large enough to accommodate a cargo plane. Or dragons preparing to launch an attack. She shivered, setting aside that thought as she turned her attention to the individuals gathered to meet them.

She smiled.

Kymri Steelscale smiled back.

Jori Mountainside stood behind her, expression grim as he watched his parents' reunion.

"Thank the dragon goddess, you are unharmed." Marli gripped her closest friend in a fierce hug. "Jori looks like shit."

"It's been a really rough few days, Mar." Kymri squeezed her back.

Beside her, Jonathan held his wife, Elora, in a similar embrace. They would have much to catch up on, after two decades of forced separation.

"What the fuck happened, Jori?" Odson growled.

Elora released her husband and approached Odson. "It's good to see you, brother."

Odson grabbed her in a bone-crunching hug. "If I'd known..."

"I know." She smiled up at him and patted his cheek.

"If you'll all follow me, there are refreshments in the new council room." A stiff dragon male said.

"Thank you, Eamerson," Jori took Kymri's hand, following the male away from the plane toward the interior of the mountain.

Marli hesitated as she observed Kymri's sure strides and Elora's grasp on Jonathan's hand, leading him inside. She wouldn't leave the only two other Aeleftherians alone in this mountain. Not her best friend, and certainly not the queen's long-lost ambassador. She spared the small plane a last glance as she trailed after them.

The male, Eamerson, led them to an elevator at the rear of the cavern. They rode it up, then followed him along several stark marble corridors to a set of black double doors.

Cold. Austere. Rigid.

Marli's nose twitched at the musky atmosphere inside the mountain.

She glanced around the expansive room that opened to a glassed-in vista of the misty mountains beyond it.

Eamerson gestured toward a table set with several trays of food and drink.

"New council room, huh?" Odson asked, sauntering toward the windows.

Marli's fingertips drifted along a seam in the glass, wondering if they opened.

The place could use a little fresh air. And a way to escape.

Marli moved to the table, reaching for the platter of cookies, gaze roaming the room and the faces within it. She ignored Eamerson, though she was mindful of his movements.

"Yes sir," Eamerson said to Odson's question. "I understand you are King Mountainside's uncle?"

King?

Cookie crumbs caught in Marli's throat, making her cough. Kymri handed her a glass of water.

Odson glanced back at her. "I am." He ran a hand through his hair and blew out his breath, turning toward Jori. "King Mountainside?"

Beside Marli, Jonathan and Elora appeared, hands linked and red-eyed.

She studied the drawn features of Aeleftheria's ambassador. "The queen will be very cross with you, for staying away after Jori's birth." Marli drew a breath. "But I know she'll be overjoyed to learn you're alive and have been rescued from Kargassa's imprisonment all these years."

Elora nodded, then shrugged as her gaze swept over her husband's face. Her throat worked as she swallowed.

It's worth it to her. And to him. After all this time.

In Marli's experience, love was fleeting, and that kind of dedication was rare.

Marli looked at Kymri. "So, what Odson said? What the fuck happened?"

Kymri briefly recounted the abduction, meeting the mountain king and the events that led to his death.

"And just like that, Jori is the new king. So what's next?"

Elora waved a hand toward the room at large. "This was Kargassa's personal space. Jori decided that turning it into a council room—like we have in Aeleftheria—would be the best use for it.

"We've asked one of the resident carpenters to make a new round table for this room."

Jonathan smiled. "You always were obsessed with Camelot, Jori."

"Kargassa wasn't the 'council' type?" Odson turned away from the windows.

"No sir. Mr. Stenlen Flintail and I acted as advisors when the previous king sought an opinion." Eamerson responded.

"Which wasn't often," Elora said.

"And the reason I asked you to come here." Jori held Odson's gaze. "I've decided to stay and try to lead this lair in a new direction, but I'm going to need help." He glanced at his watch.

Marli's gaze shot to Kymri's fingers still linked with Jori's. She swallowed. "You're not coming home, are you?"

"This is the best way to ensure Aeleftheria's safety." Kymri's free hand moved over her lower belly. "And our baby's."

Odson said, "It won't be easy turning a lair of male dragons, intent on seeking and subduing a colony of females, in a new direction."

"I agree, but he won't be alone. I am steadfast in my duty to the rightful king of this tribe. As is Mr. Flintail," Eamerson said.

Marli jerked, gaping at the male. "Flintail. Stenlen Flintail? The same male dragon that, despite my great effort to lead away from our home, still managed to find and attack it? The same male that is responsible for the two of you being dragged here, is supporting you? Seriously?" She turned on Jori and Kymri.

Jori ran a hand over the back of his neck. "Yep."

"You can't trust a rogue like that. You're insane to trust any of these males," Marli exploded. On seeing the determination in their faces, she eased back and released a breath. "Yeah, I'd say you're going to need help. The queen and her council won't like any of this. Too many of these males already know where Aeleftheria is."

Jori glanced at his watch again, then leaned close to Kymri, kissing her cheek. "I'll be right back."

Kymri said, "The queen doesn't need to know anything just yet. Besides, it's thanks to Stenlen that Elora and I are alive."

"Not tell them anything? You know I have to report back. As you should have." Marli said to Kymri, then turned to Elora again. "And you. Your disappearance broke the queen's heart. You should have seen her face when she realized Jori was your son. The council almost had him destroyed."

"Kymri told me what happened," Elora said, voice quiet. "We're still trying to get our bearings here. When you send your report, please, just don't tell them where we are. Not *yet*. Having three of us here is already going to be a challenge. We don't need the council interfering."

"You're staying, too." Marli rubbed her hands over her face and through her hair.

Elora nodded.

I'm so fucked.

"Dragonsdammit. When we left Aeleftheria, my orders were to ensure the safety of our people, find the location of the lair and to bring you both back safely. The queen ordered Kymri to eliminate Jori if he proved to be a threat to Aeleftheria. And as the king of a mountain lair full of male dragons, they're going to see him as the *biggest* threat." Marli crossed her arms over her chest, drumming her purple nails on her biceps. "They're going to be frothing at the mouth."

"Well, no one is eliminating anyone else," Odson growled, glaring at Marli.

So. Fucked.

Chapter 4

Stenlen Flintail clenched his jaw, staring the dissenter in the eyes.

He was on his way through the dining hall after lunch to meet with the new king when someone shoved him from behind. Spinning around, he growled, "Go on. Try that again." He stepped closer, despite the other male's larger frame. Sten was tall, but Frederick had the nickname 'Goliath' for a reason.

"Fucking traitor." Goliath's low voice rumbled through Sten's chest, like boulders grinding strips off of his deep sense of loyalty.

The same two words he'd heard time and again.

Sten straightened his spine. "Kargassa crossed the line."

"He was our *King*."

Sten didn't glance at the others, gathering behind Goliath.

Stenlen wasn't alone in his views. There were just as many other males that felt the same. As much as they'd wanted to take control of the Aeleftherian colony, none of them had intentions of inflicting harm just for the sake of it. There were always other ways—better ways—to dominate a female, that didn't involve maiming or death.

Which is exactly what had been at stake, and had resulted in the king's downfall.

On Kargassa's orders, Sten and his wingmen had tracked and delivered the king's heir, Jori.

The ceremony to ensure the heir's fealty and allegiance had gone terribly wrong. Kargassa had lost his patience and threatened to kill both females present—Jori's pregnant mate and his mother.

Then, the mountain lair suddenly had a new king, albeit a reluctant one.

Their home was in chaos, fracturing, exposing raw, age-old lava lines threatening to spew. The dragons were in disagreement over who should really wield the power of a king.

"And now, Jori Mountainside is our king. Rightfully acknowledged as heir by the previous king."

How many times have I said some version of that in the last few days?

Goliath snorted, stepping back from Stenlen. "Who isn't even a fucking dragon."

Until moments before the king's death, Jori had been human, then his dragon had been unleashed for the very first time.

Sten had never seen anything like it, and the mountain had been trembling with residual rumblings since.

"You were there, Goliath. He's a dragon, and he's the biggest motherfucking dragon any of us have ever seen."

"I'm big."

It was Sten's turn to snort. "Yeah, and?" He did glance at the others standing behind the Goliath now. "You plan to challenge him?"

"Why don't *you* challenge him, Sten?" One of the other guys, Randal, spoke up. "You were Kargassa's top dragon. If anyone has the right to rule this tribe, it's you. You'd be a great king. Everyone would accept you."

Sten locked eyes on him, then returned his glare to the Goliath in front of him. "I believe in the right of ascension, as do most of the other males here. I'm not Kargassa's blood kin."

"If you took one of the Aeleftherian royals, you'd have a solid claim."

Sten shrugged.

"Besides, Mountainside doesn't have the balls to bring those bitches in line. He's too much of a pussy himself." Randal said, eliciting chuckles from the surrounding males.

"Maybe. We'll see."

"Or maybe this pussy has the balls to think of something better for this tribe." Jori said from behind Sten.

Stenlen glanced behind him.

Jori leaned against the door frame, his arms across his vintage *Oasis* t-shirt, legs crossed at the ankles. He pushed away from the wall and strode toward the group, ignoring the posturing between Goliath and Stenlen.

"Eamerson tells me this place is called Kasa Kargassa."

Stenlen had been Kargassa's right-hand man—protection, scouting, tactics...muscle. Eamerson had been his left—politics, strategies...dragonkind resources.

"And?" Goliath turned his attention from Stenlen to Jori.

Sten remained at ease, but ready, in case Goliath lunged at the new king.

But Jori walked right up to Goliath, relaxed; as though he were about to ask him what his favorite snack was, and said, "And I think we should change that."

Goliath's head jerked, confusion crossed his face as he looked at Jori. "Change it? To what—Why?"

Jori shrugged, slipped his hands into the pockets of his cargo shorts as he rocked back on the heels of his combat boots. "Whatever you guys want. Because this place belongs to everyone who lives here. Not just one man—dragon."

"Damned hippie," Someone muttered.

Jori grinned. "If I was born half a century earlier, maybe."

Goliath groaned. "Kargassa left a youngling in charge. Sten, just put us out of our misery now if won't grab him by the scruff and kick him out."

Jori stepped right up to Goliath, where Sten had been, just moments before.

Sten tensed, ready to intervene.

"And you called *me* a pussy. Whine all you want, but what I will never tolerate is aggression or dominance of females. I am *not* my sire."

Sten froze, his gaze darting to each of the dragons nearby, gauging their reactions to this.

No aggression, Sten totally agreed with. But no dominance?

His gut twisted. How else were these unreasonable females going to submit and coexist peacefully with the males?

The king's woman had already stripped him down on proper addressee language.

Dragonesses were not to be addressed as bitches. Ever.

How was I to know?

Any Aeleftherian he'd paired up with before was only interested in one thing.

His dick.

Fine by him. He had more important things to do than let another bit—dragoness—wreck his heart. He'd already learned that the hard way.

Sten and most of these dragons had been under Kargassa's rule for so long, they'd become oblivious to *proper* dragon etiquette. Apparently.

Focused on finding the Aeleftherian colony—the strongest females, most worthy of powerful males like the mountain dragons, they all ignored the fact that there were other tribes out there.

Without a show of strength, how could the Aeleftherian dragonesses ever understand how to submit?

He glanced between Jori and Goliath.

This was a mistake. A big fucking mistake.

They were all going to be doomed to loneliness, with just each other's ugly faces for eternity if he didn't figure out how to sway the new king's opinion.

I'm tired of being alone.

If Sten couldn't change Jori's stance, he'd end up dead.

Chapter 5

Sten breathed a sigh of relief as Jori stepped back from Goliath.

"Let us know if you guys have any ideas on names for this place. I'm kinda partial to Oasis Cavern, or Mountain Loft. What do you think of Dragon-Man-Cave? I like that one best." He turned, grinning at Sten, and threw him a wink as he headed back toward the door.

"Those are the stupidest names I've ever heard of for a dragon lair. I can come up with ten better than those." Goliath scoffed.

"I don't know, I kinda liked..."

Sten chuckled as he followed Jori out of the mess hall. "I was on my way to meet you. You wanted to discuss the thefts?"

"I did, but that can wait. Our guests are here."

"Are you sure bringing in more outsiders at this time is wise?" They continued walking along the corridors at a brisk pace toward the elevator that led up to the king's suites.

"Absolutely. These are people I trust implicitly." They entered the elevator and Jori punched the button for the top floor.

"There are a lot of trustworthy males right here that are dedicated to your right to lead..."

Jori looked at him, his expression unreadable. "I hear you."

Sten rubbed his temple. "Can I make a suggestion?"

"Please."

"King Kargassa's body is still in the morgue. Have a ritual death ceremony that is proper for his status, and it will provide some closure for those males that believed in him."

"And give a sense of transition."

Sten nodded. "It will show them that you're not a complete outsider yourself. That you'll honor the dragon ways of doing things. He ruled a very long time, Jori, and many of us have been with him since our youth."

The doors opened; Jori led the way to the new council room.

Council room.

Things were changing. Fast.

Maybe too fast.

A familiar scent enticed his nose as he entered the vast room. His gaze swept the occupants, quickly returning to one face in particular.

His pulse accelerated as his nostrils flared.

Her.

The mists dissipated beyond the window, allowing the sun to suddenly stream through. The light caught in her caramel colored eyes, making them glow like warmed amber in her lovely face, surrounded by wild dark hair.

Their dragon scents became muted in human form. But hers was distinct and lovely, and invited him closer.

He strode toward her. "I remember you."

On seeing him, her gaze swept the length of him before resting on his face. Her perfect brows furrowed, and her chin lifted. Her lovely, full lips tightened.

This was the first time he'd been able to get a really good look at her and she was breath-taking.

Their two previous meetings had not been optimal to assess her. He'd been pursuing her in dragon form on the first occasion. And what a chase that had been! Nimble in flight, cunning in evading him. On the second occasion, it was dark, and his focus had been on keeping Odson distracted from his crew's mission to abduct Jori.

Since the mission had successfully fulfilled his orders, he understood why her expression was less than welcoming now.

He had lost himself in the beauty of her face when she suddenly pounced on him, snarling, with her claws pricking his throat.

He blinked.

Blood pounded through him, gathering below his hips.

Oh, how fierce this little bit—dragoness was!

Dragoness.

Aeleftherian dragoness.

He grinned up at her.

This one. Yes, this one is going to be my dragoness.

...If she doesn't kill me first.

Chapter 6

"Marli, I'd appreciate it if you got off of my councilman. I need you to work with him, not rip his throat out." Jori's panicked voice registered through the haze of instinct that triggered her need to subdue her enemy before he harmed her loved ones.

She shook off whoever tugged on her arm. Her human hands extended to her dazzling purple dragon claws, trained on Stenlen Flintail's muscular throat.

The rogue grinned up at her. She could sever his head from his shoulders—maybe with some effort—and he grinned at her.

"Marli!" Odson's bark cleared the last wisps of offensive need.

As she leaned back on her haunches, her bottom brushed against her enemy's hardened groin. Her nostrils flared, taking in his scent as heat ripped down through her core to meet his erection.

He chuckled, "You are a fierce one. I like you."

Marli shot to her feet, hissing and backing away from him, "Don't touch me."

Jori offered a hand to pull Stenlen to his feet.

As soon as he was upright, he put up his hands in a placating gesture, "Hey, I wasn't the one doing the touching."

Her gaze involuntarily dropped to his groin. She raised her still-clawed hands.

He was twice her size, but that didn't mean she wouldn't go down swiping and slashing if provoked.

"Marli, retract your claws. Jori's right, we need you to work with him." Kymri ordered.

At Kymri's command, Marli hesitantly obeyed.

Until recently, Kymri had been Marli's commander in the Aeleftherian guardian fleet.

"Work with him? You've got to be fucking kidding me, right? Right, Kymri? There's no way in dragons-hell that I'm experiencing this. The male funk in this place is melting my brain and I'm delusional." Marli gaped, gaze swiveling from Kymri to Jori to Stenlen and back.

"Male funk?" Jori's brows went up, nostrils flaring. "I thought it was just Kymri's pregnancy that made her sensitive to smells."

"You're not delusional. This is happening." Kymri said, hands on hips.

"I'm very hygienic," Stenlen growled, a fierce scowl souring his handsome features.

Marli flipped a hand, palm out, in Stenlen's direction, raising her own brows as she stared back at Kymri.

"Not helping," Jori said to Stenlen.

"Everyone in Black River has been driving themselves into the ground to find and rescue you from these drag-ons. And now you're all just buddies." Marli pinched the bridge of her nose as fatigue suddenly chased away the adrenaline of finally reuniting with her friend and seeing for herself that she was safe.

"She hasn't slept much since you disappeared." Odson said. "None of us have."

Kymri strode up to Marli, taking her hands in hers. "I'm sorry that you've all exhausted yourselves. And I am so thankful that you were searching for us. It was a *very* dire situation. We are incredibly lucky that things landed in our favor and we can have this meeting now." Kymri searched Marli's face. "This—being able to work together—is a good thing."

Exhausted, Marli held Kymri's direct gaze, absorbing her words.

She'd been on edge since the moment they realized she was missing, up to this very second.

Tears blurred her vision.

Blinking them away, she tilted her head up and nodded.

Her best friend, her soul sister, was safe.

That's all that matters now.

She squeezed Kymri's hands and growled, "You'd better not fucking do that to me again."

Kymri shrugged. "Can't make any promises, but I'll do my best."

"Shall we get on with this meeting?" Elora prompted.

Marli released Kymri's hands so they could focus on what the Aeleftherian Ambassador had to say.

"Now that we're here, this initial gathering is just to ensure that the core individuals have met and agree to work together." Elora's gaze landed on Marli, then on Stenlen, who stood several paces behind her.

Heat radiated from his body, caressing her back, tugging at her awareness, distracting her from concentrating on Elora's words.

Recollection of the first time she'd seen him in his human form steamrolled her brain—when she'd spent ages luring him and his wingmen away from her island and lost him on a hedonist beach.

And just how nice the sight had been.

She slammed the door shut on that memory, shifting her posture to release the sudden rush of desire, and resisted the urge to glance at him.

Elora went on, "Jori has a relationship to build with both the male dragons of this lair and with the female dragons of Aeleftheria."

Odson moved toward the large table, perching on its edge. "That'll take decades."

Eamerson nodded. "It will, and Stenlen made a timely suggestion that will accelerate the building of their trust and respect."

"Go on," Odson prompted.

"A funeral for Kargassa," Jori said, gaze locked on his mother.

Elora's mouth tightened while a vein ticked along her temple. She swallowed and nodded. "An excellent start. Upholding certain traditions is crucial."

Jonathan muttered, "He doesn't deserve it."

Marli's heart ached for the human professor. His journey these last two decades hadn't been easy, especially in recent days, with new revelations.

Without being brought to this mountain, Jori would never have found out his mother was still alive. And Jonathan would still be separated from his dragoness wife.

Elora linked her fingers with Jonathan's. "Jori needs this, so that we can avoid repetitions of what happened to us, moving forward."

Marli looked to each of the gathered faces, except for Stenlen, who remained behind her.

She moved so that she could watch him from the corner of her eye.

It was a good idea, but she didn't admit that she thought so.

Beyond them, the panorama of windows highlighted the beauty of the sunlight mountain vista. It differed vastly from her island home, but was nearly as breathtaking.

This wasn't just about ending the war between male and female dragons. This was about changing things so that there was no war at all.

And that, she would fight for.

She turned to Jori. "Where do we begin? I haven't been to many dragon funerals and I've never had to bury a monarch before."

"I've buried a few in my time," Odson nodded to Eamerson, who stood nearby with a tablet, ready to take notes.

Stenlen's voice rolled through Marli when he spoke, "I heard there's an archive somewhere in this mountain, maybe there's something in there." He spoke with the slightest of accents, that she'd never noticed before.

"Oh, there is," Eamerson looked up from the tablet. "It's accessible through the back of the library and comprises three descending levels."

"Library?" Stenlen and Marli asked in unison.

The word made Marli's heart thump.

Library.

A secret indulgence that she allowed herself any time she left Aeleftheria. Whatever town or city she landed in, she visited their collection if there was time.

Eamerson's lips twitched. "Yes, Stenlen. I will provide you the directions and what volumes to ask the archivist for while I record the notes to this meeting."

"I'll go along. You'll need help to carry the books." Marli spun toward him. She nearly laughed at Stenlen's perplexed expression. She snorted. "Never been to a library, have you?"

He shook his head.

Figures.

"Great, while you're at it, you can give Marli a tour of the place and show her where her room is while she's here." Jori said as her new guide turned toward the door. "And Sten, keep her out of trouble. In fact, stay away from the common areas, the guys—"

"I'll protect her."

"I can take care of myself."

They answered Jori's concerns at once.

Which, as a guardian and information collector, she could...

Protect me?

She cast Stenlen a sideways glance.

But maybe in the heart of male dragon territory, she might not be so cavalier about her abilities.

And maybe her impulsiveness might have just put her in a tricky situation. After all, she had just threatened him with her dragon claws.

... but a library—and an archive. A dragon archive.

Who could resist that?

Chapter 7

Stenlen glanced at the crisp card with the clean script that Eamerson handed him. The directions led to a section of the mountain he'd never bothered with.

He glanced at the dragoness walking alongside him. Spine straight, head up.

Her eyes had sparkled at the mention of a library. *Who knew?*

One moment she had her metallic purple claws to his throat—which fascinated him on so many levels—and the next she eagerly volunteered to descend into the mountain's bowels for some dusty books. With him.

He punched the 'down' button for the elevator, observing her from the corner of his eye.

She stood, feet at shoulder width, like any soldier at ease, fingers loosely linked together, with their purple nails.

The doors swished open and he stepped forward at the same time she did.

They both stopped at once.

He waved her forward, then realized manners had their perks.

She sauntered ahead of him, according him a magnificent view of her ass.

That same lovely ass that had been planted right on his groin not so long ago.

Blood flowed downward.

"Floor?" She turned toward him, brow raised.

Stepping into the elevator, he glanced at the card again and hit the listed button. It was a long way down.

Beside him, she stared at the closed doors.

In the confines of the steel box, her scent surrounded him. Infused him. Made it impossible for him to ignore her.

From that day, outside of Aeleftherian territory, when he had tracked, hunted, and failed to find her, her scent was imbedded in his memory.

He drew a slow, deep breath, savoring the silky notes that defined her unique qualities.

She reminded him of blooming tropical flowers, wild ocean tides and hot sandy beaches.

He cleared his throat. "So, that beach you led us to? You go there often?"

She slowly turned her head, looking up at him. Challenge illuminated her golden eyes. "Perhaps. A girl's gotta have some fun. It's not *all* just training and combat tactics."

"You were there, weren't you? Somewhere on the beach?" Among dozens and dozens of naked bodies, partying and enjoying the sun.

"Absolutely. I had to make sure I hadn't led you to Aeleftheria."

She hadn't. They'd found it by tracking another dragoness much later.

"That's hardly fair then, is it? You've seen me in my full human."

She shrugged, nonchalant.

He noticed the slight curl to the corner of her mouth.

She'd seen him naked, and she'd liked it.

The knowledge jolted through him.

The elevator doors swished open again. She snatched the card from his hand, taking the lead with Eamerson's directions.

That was fine with him. It wasn't like he'd been down here before, and it gave him the chance to watch her lovely ass as she strode ahead of him in search of the archive. It wasn't long before he lost himself in his own fantasies involving this little dragoness, naked, on a beach, against a wall, in his bed... even in the library, if she wanted it.

He was sure she'd be down with that...

"What?" He blinked, the images coming to a sudden halt.

"It's here." She shoved a heavily carved oak door open to reveal a vast cavern, filled with perfect rows of books upon shelf after shelf.

"Already?"

She strode right up to a wide counter and tapped the bell.

A male approached from somewhere near the back and blinked at her, brows lifted, nose twitching.

"She's the king's guest," Stenlen growled.

"Name?" The librarian shoved a thick ledger book forward.

Sten snatched a pen from the male and scribbled his name.

His gaze slid down the page, noting the names of other males who'd visited the library.

Frederick? Goliath has been here?

"We need these, thank you…" She handed Eamerson's other card to the male, peering at the nameplate on the counter beside him, and gave him a bright smile. "Sam. I just love libraries. Don't you?"

The male's cheeks flushed. He stared back with a glint in his eyes.

Stenlen growled.

The librarian's gaze shot to Sten's face, eyes round. "I'll be just a moment."

Marli turned, frowning at Sten.

"What?" He scowled back, suddenly reminded that he didn't care what she—or anyone else—thought.

What do I care if I displease her?

He reined in his rampant thoughts and desires, stamping down on thoughts of possessing her.

Maybe we'll fuck later, maybe we won't.

He examined how quickly he'd taken to wanting her. That wasn't like him.

Not anymore. Because that was dangerous.

In his youth, before Kargassa took him in, he'd had his heart broken. Shattered.

On Kargassa's advice, he'd never allowed it to mend. He gripped the jagged edges, keeping them fresh. Keeping him sharp.

Until *this* dragoness sauntered past him with her imperial glare and wicked purple claws.

Nope.

What is it about her that enticed him to drop his guard?

Not going to slip now.

Especially not with an Aeleftherian guardian.

He paced away from her as they waited for the librarian to return.

He needed the space so that her scent would stop invading his senses, his head—his blood.

That won't do. It should be the other way around.

She should be the one attracted to him, wanting to please him—wanting *him* to smile at *her.*

He strode further away, glancing over titles on the nearest shelves, with nothing better to do.

Sten even picked up a few, curious to see what was inside.

The earliest maps of dragon territories captivated him. Ancient days, from before dragon shifters hid themselves from humans. Before the division between male and female dragons, when the Aeleftherians had developed their own colony and excluded all males from their borders.

What right did they have to shut us out? Turn us away? Reject us?

Squeaking alerted him that the librarian was returning.

He snapped the book shut and jammed it back into its slot on the shelf.

Two other titles caught Sten's attention. 'The History of Kasa Kargassa' and 'King Richmund Kargassa: An autobiography.'

He snatched both books from the shelf, flipping through the pages.

When had Kargassa written an autobiography? Who wrote a history of their lair? Am I in these?

As far as he could tell, they didn't mention any dragon by name other than Kargassa himself and his forebears, establishing the dynasty.

Sten and Eamerson played crucial roles in many of his listed achievements, yet they weren't even mentioned by name.

The squeaking stopped nearby, drawing his attention.

Sten swallowed a groan as the librarian pushed a cart loaded with large tomes. He'd been hoping for a few primers.

"Thank you so much, Sam. Depending on how long I stay, I may be back," Marli said with far too much cheer as she took over the steerage of the cart, which was piled almost as high as she was tall.

"King's guests are always welcome." His gaze roamed over Marli's face, expression flat.

"Stenlen. Door."

Sten grit his teeth and strode forward, glancing at the visible titles as he passed by.

Ancient Dragon Ceremony
Intimate Dragon Relations
Dragon Etiquette
Dragon Kings & Queens
Treaties and Agreements of Dragonkind

He grunted, throwing the books he'd found onto the pile as they moved into the elevator.

Lost in thought, he ignored the tempting scent of the female next to him in the confines of the elevator.

He'd served Kargassa for most of his adult life, and he couldn't even mention him by name in his book.

It was no secret the man was self-centered, but Sten hadn't even considered the possibility that his regard for anyone that served him to be so low that he wouldn't even afford them the respect of recognition for their loyal achievements toward the successes of their tribe.

The edges of his disillusionment with his former king frayed a little more at the edges.

First, his ruthless attitude toward the females, and now this blatant disrespect for his tribe.

Belatedly, he recalled that Jori's suggestion and broached the subject.

"I'll find my room later," she said.

The elevator doors slid open.

Disheartened by the new revelation he'd discovered in the book, he trailed behind Marli as she steered the cart toward the new council room.

Council room.

Something that had not existed before Jori's arrival.

Jori hadn't ordered him to join it. He'd invited him.

Sten's gaze swept the occupants of the room.

All outsiders, except for Eamerson and himself.

Was this the right direction for the tribe?

I need to think about this.

His gaze found Marli's backside again as she pushed the cart toward the table.

I need to think about this when she's not around.

Chapter 8

Marli stifled a yawn. Stretching out her cramped muscles, she strode toward the floor-to-ceiling windows overlooking the forested valley below and the range peaks beyond.

Her brain spun with the research they'd spent hours immersed in.

The mountain history was comparable to Aeleftheria's, with the primary divergence being when the clans became enemies and continued independent of each other.

Aeleftheria had always been an island nation, but when the divide happened, females from the mountain fled seeking sanctuary. Aeleftheria welcomed them, providing protection from the dominant males intent on returning them to their lair.

A great battle saw the destruction of the island and many dragons killed.

'Never again', they'd vowed.

Marli's mother had told her the story many times over the years. Aeleftherians relocated to a secret region. A special location revealed to the queen by one of the immortals, with one condition. The realm needed to be protected from the outside world at all costs. Only Queen Regina and her council knew why this location was special.

Drawing a breath, Marli absorbed the vista before her.

Both males and females lived here at one time. Until the ego of the males grew beyond what the females would tolerate.

A shadow filled her periphery. Stenlen's scent enveloped her.

"It's beautiful," she murmured, glancing up at him.

His jaw tightened as he stared out. "It is."

His body heat was electric between them. His proximity caressed her.

I should move away.

But she didn't.

Marli's thoughts drifted to that day that he and his wingmen pursued her, trying to track her back to Aeleftheria. She recalled the sight of his dragon gliding through the sea above her hiding position on the ocean floor below.

Large, powerful, magnificent.

And then on the beach, in their human forms—among all the hundreds of naked bodies enjoying the sun and sand, she had found none as interesting and pleasing as his was.

Tall and muscled. Honed. A sure stride. Dark hair, thick lashes, a mouth for pleasure.

And other pleasurable body parts? Very nice indeed.

She shivered, also recalling the feel of him beneath her, when she'd attacked him in this very room.

Desire curled through her.

Her gaze flicked to his profile, then back to the view.

Since her arrival, she'd had to keep reminding herself that, according to Jori, Kymri and Elora, these males were no longer her enemy. These males were no longer a threat to Aeleftheria.

Aren't they?

Can I accept that?

Should I?

Just days ago, this male in particular had abducted her friend. And weeks before that, had attacked her home.

On the orders of his king. His dead king. Jori now leads this tribe, but for how long?

She cast Stenlen another glance.

Would he usurp Jori? He could. Why not? What are you waiting for?

Is he waiting for Aeleftheria to let down her guard?

But he already knew where she was. He could lead the males straight to her.

He could have at any time. So why hadn't he?

Why hadn't Kargassa ordered it as soon as they knew where it was?

Instead he'd gone after Jori. Why? What had he been waiting for?

All of this circled her mind again and again since the attack. More bits and pieces of information whirled in the chaos since her arrival, as she struggled to make sense of it.

She'd been hoping to find some answers in the books as they researched proper funerary practices for dragon monarchs.

Some hints to understanding the males, and how to protect Aeleftheria.

And through all of this, she desperately ignored the tug of Stenlen's personal scent.

This was new.

The rest of the place stank of centuries of male dragon funk, but his scent teased and drew her to him.

She'd never experienced this curious fascination with any other male she'd encountered before.

"Break time," Jori called out.

Marli spun toward the rest of the room. Stenlen remained next to her.

With bright page flags marking points of interest, Eamerson recorded the details of the books in his tablet and left them undisturbed.

"Are we making any progress?" Jori asked him.

Eamerson nodded. "I believe so, sire."

"Call me by my first name. Titles make my skin itch."

"Yes, sir."

Jori rolled his eyes. "Has anyone come across any ideas from those books as to what we should do with Clive and Merwin?"

"Clive and Merwin?" Marli's gaze swung to Stenlen. "Your goons? What do you mean 'do with them'?"

"My wingmen. They're in the dungeon until Jori decides their fate."

"Execute them?" Marli offered.

Stenlen growled at her. The energy of the sentiment rippled over her body. Confusing her as it both aroused and alarmed her senses.

She stepped toward Stenlen, scowling up into his face. "Their crimes—and yours—are clear. They attacked and abducted Aeleftherians. As did you. Were they in *our* domain, we wouldn't have wasted time before eliminating such a dire threat."

"Marli, this isn't Aeleftheria," Elora reminded her.

Marli's head jerked in her direction. Blood rushed through her system, her chest tightened. "I'm well aware, though I sense you've forgotten where your loyalties and concerns should be. They can still destroy us." Marli jabbed a finger in Stenlen's direction.

He bristled, eying the sharp purple fingertip less than an inch from his chest.

Kymri stepped in front of Marli, drawing her attention. She reached for Marli's hands.

Best of friends, able to calm one another in a heartbeat when no one else could.

"Why don't you stretch your wings? Get some air and we'll talk."

"You won't come with me?"

"I can't shift much right now, not with the little one complicating things." She swept a hand over her lower belly.

"Right. I forgot." Marli rubbed her hands over her face and through her hair, whispering. "Goddess, I'm so tired, I can't think straight anymore."

Kymri squeezed her hands before letting go. To Jori she said, "Will you show her the terrace?"

"Sure, it's right through here."

She followed him through a side room, nearly as austerely extravagant as the council room was, and only slightly smaller. The second difference was that the windows opened to a stone terrace. Glass panels slid aside, and he stepped out onto the stone. Turning, he nodded and held up a hand to someone behind Marli, signalling them to stop.

Glancing back, she saw that Stenlen stood in the doorway to the room, observing, his expression fierce.

"He's just making sure you won't try to assassinate me," Jori winked.

Marli laughed, inhaling deeply of the fresh mountain air as she joined him. "Try? Kymri wouldn't be very pleased with me if I eliminated her mate."

Her heart pounded as she surveyed the panorama. It was even more breathtaking without the glass separating them from the landscape. Her gaze halted at swaths of scarred forest. "What happened there? It looks like meteors ripped through the valley. Or a fierce dragon wrestling match."

Jori cleared his throat, rubbing a hand across the back of his neck. "That'd be me."

"Oh, that's right! I forgot that before your visit to Aeleftheria, you didn't know you were a dragon. I guess the flying lessons are a little rough?"

"Rough? That's an understatement. I'm tiring of pulling pine needles and cones out of my scales. The sap from broken branches and trunks sticks to everything. Pulling that stuff off hurts more than waxing. I'm a little more careful about not letting my ass hit certain trees."

Marli laughed all the harder. "Living on an island has its perks when teaching younglings how to fly. They learn how to swim at the same time. I can teach you a few tricks."

Jori grinned. "I have some things to discuss with Odson now, but I appreciate all the help I can get. Why don't you go for a tour around the mountains? I know Kymri is hoping you'll stay awhile, and would like you to familiarize yourself with the area."

Marli lifted a brow. "You'll trust me not to fly off straight to Aeleftheria right away and report on your mountain's location?"

Jori shrugged. "Kymri trusts you implicitly. I will too. Besides, the secrecy isn't forever. We just need a breath to figure things out, which we're hoping you'll help us do."

Guilt pricked her conscience. She'd been present for some of the discovery of his dragonhood and had seen how deeply affected he was by all of it. "Jori, what I don't understand is why these males haven't just thrown you in the dungeon and come for us."

"When your queen gives up her seat to her heir, will Aeleftherians accept the process?"

Marli nodded.

"Kargassa named me his heir in front of the entire tribe. Few question that. But, there are some that don't think I should remain on his throne because before that moment, I wasn't a dragon. It's complicated."

"And you're being cautious on handling Clive and Merwin."

"Yes. They were following the king's orders. Some guys think Stenlen is the one that should be in the dungeon because he disobeyed them. He's as loyal to this throne as you are to your queen, but he has a line his conscience won't cross." He turned away from the vista. "Get some air, and when you're ready, someone will show you to your room so you can rest."

She nodded as he left her alone on the terrace.

Even as his words tumbled through her mind, a smile tugged at her lips as she pictured his description of his attempts to fly. Shaking her head, she stripped down, stepped to the ledge and let her dragon free.

Magic shimmered as it allowed her body to expand and grow. Looking down at her toes, she admired her purple metallic claws gripping the stone beneath her paws. Stretching her wings, she launched herself out over the valley.

The fresh air and distance from the infusion of male dragon musk would give her a chance to clear her mind.

I don't know what's worse, that I'm in the midst of a male dragon lair working to help them, which seems to be so contradictory to my orders, or that I'm attracted to Stenlen.

She had been since their first encounter on the beach.

What would things be like if they didn't have the divide and enmity between them?

He didn't seem to regard her as an enemy.

Could she let her guard down and find out? *Should* she?

Decide tomorrow.

In the meantime, she considered how to word her report that was grossly overdue, and check in with Elora to confirm the best way to send it so that she didn't reveal the mountain location.

Yet.

Chapter 9

Magic fizzled over Sten's skin. It happened every time he descended to the dungeon. He rolled his shoulders to ease the tension it caused.

They were as far down inside the mountain as you could go. The elevator had stopped at its lowest level, and they'd had to descend flight after flight of stone-cut steps, well below the great hall where Kargassa had met his death, and further still.

He couldn't imagine there would be anything lower than this.

He'd overheard Kymri and Jori mentioning the power of the place. As metal and earth dragons, the earth's crust infused their natural dragon power.

"As soon as you open these doors, I'm going to fuck you up. Then I'm going after your bitches," Clive snarled.

Stenlen exchanged glances with Jori and Odson. They all stood facing Clive and Merwin through the bars of their dungeon cell.

"Fucking traitor." Merwin muttered, as he had every time Sten came to interact with them since they were imprisoned.

Odson stood, arms across his chest as he glared at Sten's former wingmen. "You two knuckleheads are doing nothing to help your case." He turned to Sten. "I always figured you were the brains of this crew."

"Fuck you, old man." Merwin paced behind Clive.

Jori rubbed a hand across the back of his neck, exasperated as he stared at the two males imprisoned behind magicked anti-dragon escape bars that Kargassa had spelled centuries ago.

Still active, the spell was attached to the Kargassa blood line rather than the dragon himself.

Was this where he got the idea for the Ambassador's collar and the manacles he'd used to subdue Kymri? Or vice versa?

"The Aeleftherians would be more than happy to take you into custody," Jori said.

"You wouldn't fucking dare," Clive spat.

Jori stepped closer to the bars. "Wouldn't I?"

Sten hadn't thought so, but in that moment, he wasn't so sure.

"The others would rip you apart."

Odson snorted. "Would they now?"

"Clive, all of your visitors are recorded. No one gets down here without permission." Sten said.

"So?"

"Four visitors. Two of which are your cousins, one you owe money to and the other is a youngling that I'm sure you've swindled into some scheme."

"That doesn't sound like a lot of support to me," Odson said, checking the edges of his nails.

Losing patience, Sten said, "Look, I told you that all you have to do is take an oath of loyalty and an oath to preserve the safety and secret of Aeleftheria's location."

"And I suppose you took those oaths? You fucking traitor."

"I told you that you're wasting your breath. You can't reason with these two." Odson said, looking at his watch.

"Yeah, it's getting late for you old man. Why don't you fuck off to your rocking chair for a nap?"

"Not a bad idea. I have a couple of sturdy ones that I made for my cabin. I'll make one for Kymri and the baby." Odson said to Jori.

"You're right, this is a waste of time." Jori said. Turning to Clive and Merwin, he said, "Your choices are the oaths where you can stay among the mountain tribe—or a blood oath, and you can both get the fuck out. Final option, I turn you over to the Aeleftherian Council, who are quite ruthless in their judgments. They were willing to execute me for accidentally landing in their territory. I'll be sending them a courtesy message after Kargassa's funeral."

"Funeral?" Merwin said, glancing at Clive. "You're holding a funeral for Kargassa? You killed him, took his throne and are now holding a funeral for him."

Jori took another step closer to the bars. "According to the ancient books, that's what good conquerors do."

"Let us go to the funeral and we'll consider your oaths. We should be there. We were his top dragons." Clive's glare slid to Stenlen.

Jori shook his head. "Take the oaths and I'll consider letting you attend. You have three days." He turned his back on them and strode toward the door.

Odson followed him.

Sten lingered. They'd given decades of their lives to Kargassa—served him together. They'd never been buddies, but they'd worked well together.

"What, Sten? What do you want?" Clive barked.

"Did either of you know Kargassa wrote an autobiography?"

Merwin shrugged. Clive shook his head. "And?"

"I came across it in the library a couple of days ago. Neither of you are mentioned in it by name. Nor am I, or Eamerson. Or any other dragon in this tribe."

"Your point?" Clive scowled at him.

It was Sten's turn to shrug. "No point. Just interesting. See you in a few days."

"Fucking traitor."

Sten didn't flinch, though it stung every time he heard it. No matter who said it.

Chapter 10

Sten stifled a yawn as he left Eamerson's office to check in on the council room before going on his daily rounds.

Most of the usual dragons, and the one human, were there.

"Where's Jori?"

Marli hadn't arrived yet either.

Kymri glanced up from Eamerson's tablet as she and Elora discussed some protocol issues. "He took Marli down to the Aerie for some sparring. They're both getting cabin fever. Neither is used to being confined for very long."

Blood drained from Sten's face. "Which part?"

Kymri shrugged.

Sten darted out of the room and mashed the elevator button.

Neither of them should be anywhere inside the mountain without him. Or at least nowhere below the top three floors that belonged to the monarch and his guests.

How many times have I warned Jori about venturing out without me?

"Dragonsdammit!" He snarled at the elevator doors, forcing patience, knowing it was still faster than running down all the fucking stairs.

Dragon form? Human form?

Jori, in dragon form, could defend himself. Marli in dragon form would be seen as a provocation. Especially if anyone saw her strip to shift.

One Aeleftherian dragoness in a mountain full of males...

He swallowed.

In their human forms, they were both vulnerable if someone decided to have a go.

By the time he reached the Aerie's floor, he was sure he'd find them both ripped to pieces by the faction that Sten had yet to convince to accept the new king—despite the oaths they had taken.

The doors swished open and Sten was sure he lost a layer of skin as he forced himself between the too-slow doors and sprinted through corridors that echoed with shouts.

Fuck. I'm too late.

Sten had to shove his way between males to reach the center. Heart hammering in his throat, he gasped for breath, taking in the scene.

Musk, sweat and testosterone hung heavy in the air.

There *was* a funk surrounding them.

Marli, in too-big sweats with the sleeves and ankles rolled up, faced Jori, shirtless, shoe-less, wearing his cargo shorts. They both wore sparring gear, bouncing on the balls of their bare feet, circling one another.

Even her toenails were painted purple to match her fingers.

Marli spun, foot shooting out and up. Jori blocked it with a gloved hand and swung with the other.

She danced away, feinted and swung her foot low, taking his feet out from under him.

He fell hard on the mat.

"Oh!" the crowd said in unison.

Sten gaped at the onlookers.

No one looked like they were going to attack. They were all too engrossed in the sparring match.

The grip on his chest muscles eased, and he breathed a little deeper.

He took the moment to observe a little longer.

He noted where Jori could use more training, but his attention constantly slid back to Marli.

Controlled, creative, tactical. Fast.

Which was why she could evade Sten, Clive and Merwin when they'd gone after her that day.

Every male in this place towered over her, making her a vulnerable target.

I need to get them back upstairs before the males get bored.

He listened carefully between the shouts, urging one or the other to hit a target or take their opponent down. Some even called for Jori to ease up on Marli, which, he noted, seemed to make her come at Jori with more force.

Jori blocked most of the strikes but took a few jabs to the ribs.

Raised voices to Sten's right drew his attention.

"Hey, that's mine!" One male gripped the shoulder of another.

Sten moved in closer to sort out what was going on. They appeared to be arguing over a thick gold bracelet.

"What the fuck, man? You sold it to me yesterday." Pete said.

"Are you high? It went missing two days ago and I haven't seen you in a week." Craig said.

"Am I high?" Pete gaped, then turned to his friend engrossed in the sparring match, shoving his shoulder to get his attention. "Den, where did I get this?" He held up the bracelet.

Den's expression registered confusion, but he answered, nodding to Craig. "Craig sold it to you yesterday in the mess hall. Fair price too. I'd have asked for more."

"I've been on duty in the dungeon all week and haven't had time to sell my shit in the mess hall."

"If you want it back that badly, just give me back my money."

Craig git his teeth, growling. "I don't have your money because I didn't sell it to you."

Stenlen intervened before the conflict turned physical in the crowded area. "How about you take this matter to Eamerson. He's in his office at the moment. Fourth floor." He jerked his head toward the exit.

They glowered at each other, but obeyed the order.

This was the fourth instance of similar miscommunications in as many days.

Scanning the crowd, he moved toward any male that appeared to be plotting—or leering.

"I'd take *that* down on the mat anytime," one male said, eyes roaming over Marli as she nimbly dodged Jori's swings.

"You and me both, brother."

The first chuckled. "As long as I'm first."

Sten slid in front of him, blocking his view of Marli, holding his gaze as he growled. "Show some respect toward our royal guest, and representative of an ally nation."

The male's brows shot up at Sten's unexpected appearance and aggressive reaction. "I was just kidding, man."

"Let's go," his friend turned to leave. "He's just got a hard-on for her himself and doesn't want any competition. Or company."

Sten growled louder. They both quickly left.

The third group he encountered didn't leave him with any less worry.

"See how he's leaning? Stance is wrong. He's got some training, but he isn't adept enough to sustain a true fight. It would be easy to take him down. The bitch on the other hand, she's very well trained and is obviously going easy on him. But she's small. Separated from the other bitches? Easy. Cornered? Done."

Sten listened a little longer as they continued to assess the new king and his guest, learning what he could of their attitude and intentions.

They took the oath. Are they just all talk?

He considered assigning a deputy to monitor this group.

Their conversation turned to a race they were looking forward to watching on the big screen in the common room.

His gaze passed the tunnel that led to the larger section of the Aerie where the dragon sparring happened.

His nose twitched as fresh air drifted toward him.

Drawn, he moved toward the entrance, watching as two teams practiced aerial combat.

It was a cavern that opened to a sheltered gully, enclosed by the mountain range curling around itself. The ground was littered with thousands of snapped scales, broken claws and teeth, a torn back ridge or two, and dozens of tail barbs.

He sighed as his thoughts turned back to Clive and Merwin. Just weeks ago, they had trained together, pitting themselves against some of these guys to stay fit and sharp.

I need a new team.

He watched the dragons as they twisted and wrestled.

Would any of them ever trust me enough to have their back again?

He seemed to have Jori's trust, which meant a lot. But was it enough if he didn't also have the trust of his tribe?

He blew out a breath and turned his back on the Aerie to escort his king and their guest back up to the safety of the upper suites.

Time to think about that later. Too many fires to put out now.

Sten found a gap in the crowd and waited until he eventually caught Jori's attention. He signaled they should get back.

Jori acknowledged with a nod, releasing his stance. "Time to get back to work!"

Marli straightened and removed her sparring gear.

The crowd grumbled, but dispersed.

Sten moved closer as several males approached the pair.

He smiled, hearing them offer their king some pointers and Marli a few compliments.

Sten had to admit. It was pretty ballsy of both of them to come down here.

Kargassa had never engaged in sport. His appearances before the tribe were always surrounded with pomp and ceremony. The dragons rarely saw their king.

No, Jori certainly was *not* his sire.

Chapter 11

"Jori, you don't have to participate in the fly-by." Kymri called down from the ledge of the terrace, trying to stop him from having another go. The wind whipped her red hair around her pale face.

Jori, in his dragon form, clung to the side of the mountain just below the terrace.

Marli bit her lip. She had to admit—it was pretty bad; she wouldn't have believed it had she not seen it for herself.

He'd been aiming to land on the terrace and hadn't quite made it.

Goddess, I can't believe the windows haven't shattered from an impact so close!

He was the biggest frikking dragon she'd ever seen in her life. Bigger than Odson. The sheer size of him made her heart pound and she was nearly knee-droppingly thankful to the goddess that he was on their side.

Had Kargassa succeeded in turning him to his own devices... no, she wouldn't even think about it.

But, a massive dragon that didn't know how to use his wings? No wonder the valley was ripped apart.

At least this was a section of the mountains that wasn't inhabited—as far as anyone knew.

If it had been, it likely wasn't anymore.

"Just take a little break. Twenty minutes. Then you can go back out." Kymri shot Marli a wide-eyed glance. "I'll ask Odson to bring you in."

His growl reverberated along the stone.

Kymri threw up her hands. "Okay, fine. I won't."

"I'll go back to the council room," Marli volunteered.

At Kymri's nod, Marli made her way inside and through to the books that still lay strewn across the tables, with their page flags and sticky notes.

Two of her favorite human inventions, alongside the discovery of coffee and chocolate.

"Have you found the proper procedure for the order of which banners go where yet?" she asked Odson, who stood by the windows, holding a large tome over each forearm and squinting at the scripts.

"No, I left that for Eamerson. He likes that sort of detail. I'm looking for something else."

She sidled up to him, peering at the pages. "What is it?"

"I read something in Kargassa's autobiography—don't bother, by the way, it's mostly fiction as far as I can tell. But this one section caught my eye, so I'm trying to cross reference it."

"Which is?"

He leveled his gaze on her face for a long moment, undecided if he should tell her.

The hairs on her nape rose. "What is it, Odson? What's wrong?"

"I'm not sure yet. I need to find an old map of the dragon territories. Old, from before Aeleftheria's relocation."

"There's one in the library. I was looking at it while we were waiting for Eamerson's list." Sten said, leaning across the table for the bowl of mixed nuts.

"I'll get it. What's the title?"

Sten shrugged, popping several nuts into his mouth.

"Where was it?" she huffed.

"I'll go. I'll know it when I see it again." He brushed his hands clean and turned for the door.

Glancing back toward the other room, she rushed toward the elevator, murmuring, "I think we can get back before Jori does so that we don't miss what Odson has to say."

Sten caught up to her, hitting the button before she did.

In the last few days, they'd kept their distance, working alongside the others to plan the funeral as efficiently as possible.

Time, and solid sleep, had allowed her to adjust to the new situation, observing Stenlen, observing the others around him. And Eamerson too, and the various deputies that came and went.

Marli, Kymri, and Elora were warned against venturing out alone until things were settled.

While she'd enjoyed the sparring session with Jori and desperately needed the physical release, she'd been on edge, and questioned the sanity of their actions.

It had been his idea, and it was nearly impossible to resist the spark in his eyes at the potential mischief.

Eamerson had loaned her his sweats and off they'd gone.

She hadn't had that much fun in a long time and it felt good to blow off the stress of the past weeks.

What she hadn't expected was Sten's lecture on the dangers of going around the mountain without him during the elevator ride up.

She glanced at him again as they waited for the steel doors to slide open.

They stepped into the elevator. She pushed the button to the floor they needed.

The library doesn't count as 'going out alone', does it?

His head turned slightly as he looked down at her from the corner of his eye.

Heat emitted from his body as he stood next to her, rippling along her arm.

She no longer reacted to him as an enemy, but she hadn't let her guard down, either.

Her inner dragon was drawn to him more and more.

They stood inches apart in the center of the steel box.

Not just my dragon.

She was surprised to find that she not only tolerated his presence, but actually enjoyed it. Every time they were in the same room, she found herself looking for him.

And when she did, he was often already looking at her, or if he wasn't, he quickly met her gaze.

Her nostrils flared, taking in his scent. A scent that she recognized immediately, and lately noticed that she inhaled a little deeper when he was around.

She watched him move—at first, to keep an eye on where he was at all times. Now? Because she savored the sight of him as he moved around the room. Bunched muscle, ready to pounce, like any hunter or warrior. The way they countered each other in a room reminded her of a dance.

Watchful, dangerous, graceful, sensual.

By the time the elevator doors opened, her heart beat a little faster.

He followed her out.

Her senses homed in on him, fully aware of where he was.

At the grand oak library door, he reached forward to open it for her.

"It shouldn't take long to find." His deep voice rolled through her, sounding husky.

She met his eyes.

Does he feel it too?

"You seem to really like this place. Shall I take my time locating the book?" His eyebrow flicked roguishly as a smile tugged at his lips.

Her gaze lingered on his mouth, then swept the vast library. "I'd be happy to let you take all the time you need, but Odson seemed anxious."

The librarian wasn't at his desk.

"Odson can wait." Sten strode toward the shelves she'd seen him at before.

She joined him, perusing the titles. Marli gasped, pulling one from the shelf, running her palm over the embossed title. "We have a copy of this one in our own library. And these." Her finger drifted along the spines of a collection.

Sten moved closer to peer at the titles she pointed out. Her breath hitched at his proximity.

She turned her back to the shelf, cradling the book she still held. "I've read this one so many times. It has all the old stories of dragon heroes and heroines from ancient times."

He glanced down at the book, then into her eyes. "Your eyes light up when you come in here."

"Do they?" She held her breath as his eyes roamed her face.

He nodded, leaning a little closer. "Your whole face does, too."

He stood so close that she had to ease back against the shelf, her head leaning on the leather bound spines, while looking up at him. "What makes you light up?"

He paused, his gaze suddenly turning very intense. Smiling, he said, "Beautiful women with luminous caramel eyes and wild hair that love dusty libraries." He braced his hands on the shelves above her head.

"It's not dusty in here," she murmured, lost, as he leaned closer.

His lips descended toward hers.

She rose on tiptoe to meet him.

One hand still clutched the book to her chest, the other grasped his shirt, pulling him closer to her as desire scorched through her veins.

She wanted him.

He didn't touch her except with his lips.

She wanted more.

Opening to him, his tongue slid across the tip of hers, teasing.

She let go of his shirt, her hand finding purchase on his nape, anchoring him in place as she rose to meet him.

He still didn't touch her.

"May I be of service?" The librarian's voice broke the spell, drawing her attention.

"No," she snapped.

"No," Stenlen said, holding her gaze, his own eyes now alight as he smiled down at her. "I have exactly what I came for." He pulled a book from the shelf next to her head.

She released her grip on his neck, snatching her hand back as though he'd scalded her.

Her cheeks flamed. "Rogue," she muttered, and slithered her way out of the space she'd been only too happy to make even smaller just seconds before.

His chuckle followed her out of the library.

Chapter 12

Sten swaggered along behind Marli, enjoying the view of her luscious ass. He no longer had any doubt that he'd get her into bed. And soon.

After days of hedging and watching, he'd learned to give her space, pretending to ignore her.

In reality, it had been a challenge to focus on the research they were supposed to be doing in favor of fantasizing about how he was going to enjoy her charms.

The two books he had taken a serious interest in were Dragon Etiquette—after Kymri had alluded that that existed—and Intimate Dragon Relations, which detailed dragon physiology and mating traditions. Most of it was bullshit, but he could see how it might be effective.

So, he experimented. Between the two books, he was making some headway toward reducing Marli's skittish, claw-threatening attitude.

He'd also discovered that the more she relaxed around him, the more he enjoyed having her around.

His goal had changed from 'just a good fuck' to actually having her like him.

And in order to do that, he had to set aside his expectations, observe, and maybe put some effort into being likable.

Practicing etiquette had great perks.

Not snarling and growling at everything that displeased him, as was expected in a male-dominated domain. Females viewed that as threatening.

Looking her in the eyes, which, if he wasn't careful, would get him lost in their amber glow, lit by her blinding smile.

Once, he heard her laugh, and tried to think of ways to hear it again.

He had thought he wanted to dominate her, and abhorred the idea that she might want to do the same to him.

Now?

He didn't like the idea of domination so much as mutual lust.

The delight in her face over that book had been too much, and the urge to kiss her blocked every other thought in his brain, though he'd dimly noted the title he'd been there to find was right by her head.

Still, he had leaned in, drawing her scent deep into himself.

She smells so fucking sweet. I can't get enough of her.

And her taste. His mouth on hers, drinking her in. Intoxicating.

It's just as well the librarian broke the spell, otherwise I'd have taken her right there against the shelf.

It took him a moment to breathe and try to control the blood rush to his dick.

He reflected on the overwhelming instinct to have her. The desire to make her his—but not just in the sexual sense.

Stenlen wanted more. The need for more of her pounded through his heart.

The need to protect her.

His need to be the one to make her smile and the one to taste her lips.

The only one to make love to her, when the time was right.

He still examined his old self. The youngling self that had gotten his heart ripped apart and hedged that sense of devotion and single-minded adoration.

I haven't been that dragon in a long, long time.

He also examined his more recent self, after decades of remaining separate from everyone else, as Kargassa had advised, as 'the best way to control every situation to your benefit.'

Sten lately realized that Kargassa knew what he was talking about because it was like a pyramid. His subordinates were isolated and focused on their duty—to him.

Sten had been called 'traitor' so many times in the weeks since Kargassa's fall that it was starting to roll off his scales. He had disobeyed his king. Technically, he *was* a traitor. And he still warred with himself over this.

The new king didn't expect absolute loyalty in the same way Kargassa had.

Nor was he weak.

Sten had pledged loyalty, but he still watched and analyzed the new dragon on the throne, questioning if he'd made a mistake. He still wasn't sure—except when he considered Marli, and what Kargassa's plans for her people meant. The longer he worked alongside the Aeleftherians, the better he understood them. His respect for the females grew.

They weren't so different in most things.

Can we make this fanciful dream work? Bring peace between the two tribes? Time will tell.

For now, he'd do his due diligence where his tribe was concerned.

He was pleased that Jori acted on his advice about the funeral and had thrown so much time and effort into it. The effects were rippling through the mountain. The males were talking, assessing, gossiping about what it all meant. What would happen next? When would the other shoe drop? With Kargassa, there was always something else.

Sten remained the eyes and ears for the king. The more he helped Jori, the more Marli seemed to accept him.

His gaze swept her again as they rode the elevator up. He stood slightly behind her. Now and then her head would turn, as though locating him. His hands itched to touch her. To slide over her shoulders, down her arms, and around her waist.

To pull her into his arms.

He couldn't remember the last time he'd held some-one—or been held—in such an intimate way that wasn't just fucking.

He resisted the impulse to brush her hair from her nape and plant kisses along the curve of her neck and shoulder.

Sten was so hard for her, breathing was difficult.

Especially after that kiss.

He thought he'd been in control. Until she opened to him, gripped his neck and all he could think about was giving her anything she wanted, that would make her even hotter for him. He'd hand her every fucking book in the library if it meant she'd turn that luminous gaze on him.

He suddenly realized it wasn't just his balls that were aching.

His heart ached, too.

Stenlen really didn't want to be looking at the other male dragons for the rest of his life. He also wasn't thinking of any other female dragon he'd known over the years, either.

Just Marli.

Since her arrival.

Since she'd pinned him to the floor and threatened to rip out his throat, hers was the only face he'd thought about since. At first, it was mostly her ass. Then both equally. Now, he realized he thought of her face more, especially when she smiled.

And now he had the feel of her soft lips and the taste of her tongue to add to that delicious list. He was beginning to understand that her scent had imprinted on him long ago, during that very first encounter. And he'd lost her. Had fate brought her back to him?

The elevator doors slid open. She stepped forward, then paused. Over her shoulder she said, "If you have any books you'd like to talk about, you know where my room is."

She strode away.

His fist shot out to stop the doors from closing.

Hell yeah!

His new favorite book was Dragon Intimate Relations. He could tell her all about it. Better yet, show her all the drawings he'd memorized.

Books are fucking awesome.

Chapter 13

Marli handed Stenlen's book to Odson, glancing briefly at the title to see that it was a historical atlas of some kind. The leather binding was thick and crackled, the pages deeply yellowed, with their edges crumbling.

She noted Kymri had lured Jori inside with Odson's new mystery.

Elora and Jonathan also joined them.

"That one, too?" Odson asked, nodding to the other book she still clutched to her chest.

"This one's just ancient dragon mythology."

Turning, he set the old tome on a tabletop. His large, scarred hands were gentle as he handled the vellum pages.

To Marli, that right there was Odson. Large and scarred, but ever so gentle when it mattered most.

He was Jori's biological uncle, but Marli viewed him as her own surrogate uncle as well.

Many of the younger Aeleftherians did, even though he rarely set foot on the island.

He was a living legend, and nearly everyone sought him out when they went adventuring off-island to the continent.

She smiled to herself. He acted more like a doting aunty to everyone, than the hardened old warrior that he was.

"Here it is." He tapped the page with a trim, clean fingertip.

"What is?" Jori leaned over the table to see the map Odson pointed at.

"The old territories?" Stenlen leaned in too.

"Have you been in Kargassa's vaults yet?"

"Vaults? No. There hasn't been time to inventory his treasure hoard with everything else we've had to do; keeping the peace, ensuring oaths, following up on who's still here and who's left…who's determined to take my head, versus who might protect it. You know." Jori shrugged.

"Long winded, but okay. Clearly you need some time away, Jori."

Jori's lips compressed. "Yeah, that would be nice. Anyway. The vaults?"

"I think this is important—not urgent, mind you, but I'll have to talk to some folks." Odson drew a breath, lining up his thoughts. He turned to Elora. "Did mom tell you the old stories? The really old ones, from before the divide?"

"The myths?" She nodded at Marli's book. "Of course. I was very young, but every Aeleftherian heard those stories."

The hair rose all over Marli's body. Odson was excited about something to do with the myths and the old days.

She never saw him excited. About anything, ever. Her heart pounded, waiting for him to get to his point.

"I finally finished reading Kargassa's autobiography."

"Odson, you're all over the place."

"Bear with me here." He pointed at the map, with a mountain at its center. "Aeleftheria has always existed in some form or place. But before the divide, many of her inhabitants lived here, at the mountain."

"Okay." Marli nodded.

"In Kargassa's book, he mentioned a young dragon that joined the tribe some decades ago. This young dragon introduced Kargassa to a group he called the Consortium. Kargassa boasted about how this group of self-proclaimed liberators sought an alliance with him. He wined and dined them, learned what they were all about, drew them in, bringing them to the edge of agreement. Played them. Then he turned them away."

"You said that book was mostly fiction."

"It is. Mostly. The Consortium is real. It's complicated. The point is, that he said they'd discovered that the mountain dragon lord held what they thought was some kind of key."

"So, what does this key open?"

"I don't know, but I know someone who might."

"What does it look like?"

"Don't know that either."

"So, there may or may not be some kind of key which we don't know what it looks like, stored in the vaults, based on a potentially fictitious recounting of an obscure group of liberators."

"Sounds about right." Odson nodded.

Jori rubbed a hand over the back of his neck. "Right. Okay. That's cool, but what does this have to do with anything that's happening now?"

"First," Odson held up a finger. "The same person who might know about the key has also been tracking Consortium activities for centuries."

"Centuries—" Jori gaped.

"Second," Odson went on. "My gut tells me there's a connection between you being brought here, once Kargassa had learned the location of Aeleftheria Nisi." Odson turned to Stenlen. "He didn't invade."

Stenlen shook his head. "I advised him to plan the invasion to gain overlordship of the female colony. That's what he'd always said was the goal. Instead, he told us to pick up this vlogger he'd been following on-line." Sten nodded at Jori.

Jori's expression turned morose as he blew out a breath.

"You didn't know. How could you have?" Kymri slipped her arm around his waist.

"So it's true? You found our island because you tracked Jori's vlog to the Bermuda Triangle?" Marli looked from Stenlen to Jori.

"Yes. I just had no idea *why* Kargassa was following his show."

"I still don't get how any of this is linked, Odson?"

"The Consortium are myth chasers, too. But unlike you, they're mostly underground, and while they referred to themselves as liberators, they're quite the opposite. They've proved themselves to be exploiters and extortionists to get what they want. And they're very careful about who they reach out to."

"Given Kargassa's nature, they had to be sure the thing existed, let alone where it was." Sten nodded.

"Still, you said that was decades ago." Jori looked between the two.

"Right. And Kargassa is unexpectedly dead. The mountain is unstable. I expect they'll reach out again."

"Do you know who's come to the mountain over the years?" Jori asked, peering over Elora's shoulder at the atlas.

"Some. Kargassa kept us busy, so I didn't spend much time with newcomers. That was more Eamerson's department."

"What do you propose?" Elora asked, looking up from the map depicting the old territorial boundaries.

Odson turned to Jori. "I know you asked me here to help build your new council. I will help with that but—"

"Your gut is telling you there's something in this, and you need to take off."

Odson nodded.

"I agree," Elora said. "Kargassa may have engineered all of this from the very start, Jori."

Marli swallowed at Elora's taut expression. Her heart went out to the Ambassador and her complicated past with the mountain tribe. Jonathan slid his fingers between Elora's. He hadn't left her side since their reunion.

"He just never accounted for the event that you wouldn't submit," Stenlen said to Jori.

"Or that I'd kill him." Jori nodded, reaching for his mother's free hand.

"Aeleftheria needs to know about this," Marli's soft voice pulled Elora's gaze.

Elora nodded.

Odson put up his hands. "Just—just let me get more information first. We need more before taking this to the queen."

Exasperated, Marli said, "The report I sent after I got here was short and vague and they're going to want to know why I haven't returned yet. The queen and council have a right to know about this other threat."

Odson nodded. "For now. The Consortium reached out to the mountain dragons and I expect they will again as soon as word gets around that Kargassa is dead. And with males leaving here, it will."

"Let's deal with the funeral first. We need to stabilize the mountain tribe before we deal with outsiders that may eventually come," Elora said.

"As soon as that's handled, I recommend that you read Kargassa's book, study the maps, and look at Marli's book of myths. There may be clues." Odson nodded toward Marli, still clutching the book from the library.

"When are you going?"

"Now."

"So soon," Marli breathed.

"You don't need me here for the funeral."

"It would be a powerful show of support to have you at Jori's back during the ceremony," Elora said.

Odson considered this. "Maybe. Having Stenlen and Eamerson behind him will be a stronger statement. I can be of better use outside the mountain."

"Because you don't intend to stay here anyway," Jori said.

Odson shook his head.

The disappointment was palpable in the room. Not just from Jori, but from everyone there. But no one tried to argue Odson's decision.

"You always were a wild card." Elora reached up to pat Odson's cheek. "Don't stay away too long, brother."

Odson gripped her fingers, kissing her hand. "Visit me at Black River, Elora. Heidi would love to see you again."

There was nothing more to say other than share their goodbye-for-nows, and hugs in some cases.

He left the council room for the terrace and was gone.

Marli rubbed her hands over her face and back through her hair. "That was intense. I feel like I'm not quite sure what just happened there." Everyone else seemed to share the sentiment.

"I need some air," Jori said.

Kymri's expression turned pained as she dropped her voice. "I can't help if you get into trouble again. My shifting is too unstable now.

"I can do with some air, too. Mind if I join you?" Marli strode forward, slinging an arm across Kymri's shoulders. "We've all been cooped up in here too long."

Jori grinned at Marli. "Oh! Yeah, you can teach me how to do the barrel rolls I saw the guardians do. Kymri refused to—"

"No!" Kymri and Sten said at once, shaking their head.

"What?" Jori said, eyes wide and innocent. "It'll be fine."

Chapter 14

Sten had flown with Jori before. A bunch of times now.

He drew a deep breath and let it out slowly, rolling his shoulders.

Jori needed to learn. That's all there was to it.

"I'll go first, you follow. We need to already be in the air so that he has room to launch, and in case there's trouble." Sten instructed Marli.

Jori rolled his eyes. "It's not that bad anymore, Sten."

"Anymore." Sten gave Jori a meaningful look.

Marli laughed. "Don't be so dramatic. He was doing okay earlier."

"Marli, he can't land."

"He just hasn't seen the right technique."

"Technique? I supposed that's *your* technique, right?"

"Of course," she shrugged, eyes aglow.

"Guys, I'm right here." Jori complained. "I've almost got the landings right."

"It's crucial, *sire*. Otherwise, there won't be any mountain left for you to rule." Sten grumbled.

"Low blow, Sten."

"Well, you two can squabble all you want. I need to stretch my wings."

With a glance, Jori turned his back to Marli as she pulled her shirt up over her head and dropped onto the stone ledge. The rest of her clothing followed in succession.

Sten's breath caught in his throat. He dry swallowed as he appreciated her curves.

"Sten," Jori barked, noticing that he was gaping at their guest.

Sten reluctantly turned from the lovely view to gaze out over the mountain range while she shifted.

The fizzle of her magic tickled his skin. The only sound that followed was the swish of her wings as she launched into the sky.

He was still watching when Jori cleared his throat. "You going out or you staying to spectate?"

Sten snorted as he pulled his shirt off and laid it next to Marli's clothing. He paused, noting the bright green lace thong abandoned on the haphazard pile.

"Sten," Jori's voice pulled his attention again.

"Yes?"

"She's my girlfriend—my future queen's—closest friend."

"Understood."

Jori nodded and gestured for him to proceed.

As soon as he was airborne, he ascended, joining Marli's overhead circling.

Sten never tired of feeling the wind under his wings, the view from the greatest heights and the cleansing scrub of the purest air.

The sun glinted off of her shiny purple claws and gorgeous scales. She was small and lithe and built for speed. He already knew how nimble she was, to have eluded him and his wingmen during their previous chase.

He suddenly wished he could change those first encounter circumstances—take her to another beach where they could be naked together. Alone or not, he didn't care.

Her dragon scent filled his nose as he flowed through her trail, igniting his hunter's instinct. He savored her unique blend as it slid over his tongue and across his flared nostrils.

Perfect.

Movement below drew his attention back to his novice king.

He marveled that the terrace could support his size.

Jori's long neck craned as he checked his position, ensuring his tail wouldn't shatter the windows when he launched, though they always shook from the force of the wind from his powerful wings.

Kymri, Elora, and Jonathan monitored from the council room windows.

Jori ascended to match their height and began the routine that they'd established, allowing him to strengthen his control.

Once through all of that, they began a game of chase.

Marli's proximity continually distracted Sten from watching Jori's movement. Still, he forced himself to focus, giving the signals the king needed when his positioning was off.

After some time, Marli went whizzing across his path.

What the—?

The second time she did it, he nipped the end of her tail as she blurred past him.

Oh, no you don't...

The third time, she evaded him, flicking his chin with the tip of her tail.

Sten bolted after in pursuit, determined to meet her challenge.

He nearly had her when she suddenly banked upward and barrel rolled, swooping down across his path again, forcing him to veer left.

Damn, she's agile!

She circled Jori in an upward spiral.

He turned and followed.

Shit!

Sten's wings thrust downward with all his strength, launching himself forward. He was too late to cut across Jori's path to divert him from climbing into the upper atmosphere.

Shit! Shit! Shit!

Kymri's going to have my ass if I don't stop him!

While Sten was fast and strong, he lacked Marli's maneuverability.

Jori even less so. And he still wasn't used to the size of his dragon form, which meant that he constantly misjudged his dimensions.

Sten gave chase as Jori climbed, following Marli's elegant spiral.

He even mimicked her arch and bank perfectly.

Sten drew breath to give a sounding blast to bring them both to their senses.

Play time was officially out of hand.

Jori *could* fly. What he could *not* do, was land.

He watched, helpless as Marli executed another perfect barrel roll and smoothly banked out of it before she was anywhere near the mountain tops.

Jori's turns were much wider, occupying vaster amounts of sky.

Oh no.

Sten hovered, horrified.

Jori tilted into a free-falling spin that quickly sounded like a freight train barrelling toward the mountainside—where the council room perched.

Sten clearly saw Kymri mouth 'fuck' before she spun to shove Elora and Jonathan away from the windows.

Everything happened in slow motion. Sten scrambled forward at the same moment Marli did.

Jori came out of his spin, massive wings snapping open like sails caught on a hurricane. He teetered, catching himself, but couldn't hold the position as he put his feet out to grasp a swathe of rock.

Marli's slight form torpedoed in, bouncing Jori away from the council room windows, while Sten did the same from the opposite direction.

It was enough to avoid the massive glass wall.

Jori scraped his way up the mountain peak. Boulders tumbled, trees snapped, the lair's communications tower crumbled.

There is absolutely no fucking way I'm going to let him do the fly-by at the funeral.

Sten drew a deep breath, then let it out slowly as he flew forward to assess the damage done to his king.

Sten landed on the fresh mountain scar, Jori nowhere to be seen.

Marli flapped overhead.

After a moment, Jori climbed out of a nest of broken trees. "Marli, that was fucking awesome!" he gave a thumbs-up to the dragoness. "Sten, I'm in a fuck-ton of trouble, and I've got tree sap on my balls again."

Sten sighed, lowering his foreleg so Jori could climb up.

That's what happens when an extreme adventurer becomes King of the Mountain.

Chapter 15

Marli snickered as Kymri's rant continued.

"Are you laughing, Marli?" Kymri spun, face flushed, red hair a mess, finger extended.

Marli erupted with a full out snort-laugh. "You are going to be a formidable mother, Kymri."

"This isn't funny!" Kymri's arms dropped to her sides.

"Yes, yes, it is Kym."

On seeing her friend's exasperation, Marli did her best to curb her mirth.

"But you should have seen him. He executed that barrel roll perfectly! It was just the—"

"The landing. I know." Kymri crossed her arms, glaring at Marli. "What's the damage this time?"

"Mostly just trees and rock face."

"Mostly?" Kymri arched a brow.

"Sten said something about a communications tower beyond repair."

Kymri threw up her hands, turning away.

Jori appeared in the doorway, looking sheepish.

Marli took that as her sign of a rescue departure. "It's all good, Kym. They'll replace it and we'll get on with the important stuff." She skipped out before Kymri could gear up for another rant.

"I see you still have your skin," Sten said from outside the door.

"Barely. I haven't seen her that mad in a very long time. She's always been the cool-headed one." Marli shrugged as she continued walking. "I guess pregnancy does that."

Sten fell in step alongside her. "You're right though, that was a spectacular barrel roll. Incredible flying. Especially that last bounce to keep him out of the council room." He nudged her shoulder.

She glanced up at him. Heat warmed her cheeks under his praise. "Thanks."

They continued on until they reached the door to her room. "Seeing you in flight again reminded me of that first time we met."

She turned, lifting a brow. "Seeing you naked also reminded me of that first time."

He gave a short laugh, scratching at his temple with his thumb. "Ehm, well, that's not what I was referring to."

"Your flying was pretty impressive, too." She smiled up at him, reaching out to smooth the collar of his shirt. "Are you coming in?"

His dark eyes flicked between her face and the door. He frowned as he considered his words.

"Sorry," she blurted. "Just forget that. Not appropriate. Didn't happen." She turned to go into her room, but he caught her arm.

"I'd like to, but I need to say something first."

She swallowed, studying his face. Since she'd been there, she'd never seen him so... solemn? Unsure?

She bit her lip, breath held.

His throat worked, and he licked his lips before he spoke. He lifted his eyes and held her gaze.

Direct, raw, honest.

"I-uhm. I'm sorry we were so relentless in pursuing you. Three males, each more than twice your size. That had to have been harrowing for you. And... also that we attacked your home. Everything you fought to defend, to protect, is upside down and at risk because of us—me. Because of me."

Speechless, heart racing, she nodded and drew a slow breath. "Thank you, Stenlen."

"I just thought you should hear that from me." He turned to go, but she caught his hand this time.

His fingers were warm and strong. He didn't pull away. Looking down at their joined hands, he slid his fingers along hers.

She shivered and inhaled his scent. "You smell nice."

He leaned closer, as though drawn by the intake of her breath. "I thought you said we stank." The corner of his lips lifted as he drew ever nearer.

"Funk. This place has a funk. But not you."

"No?" His lips were inches from hers.

Her pulse stammered. It was like the library all over again.

"You're very hygienic," she murmured.

Reaching behind her, she turned the door handle so that it swung open.

He didn't glance at it. He dipped his head close to her collarbone, a breath from her skin. Sten inhaled, slow and steady, along the crook of her shoulder and up along her neck, stopping just below her ear. "I like how you smell, too."

Oh, dear goddess!

She shivered with a gasp as moisture soaked her panties and her nipples peaked.

Dragonsdammit, he was so hot and he made her scorch... he hadn't even touched her.

"Do you want to talk?" his lips ghosted hers, just the heat of him glided along the sensitive flesh.

"Talking is okay," she whispered.

Footsteps from somewhere around the corner echoed along the marble corridor.

Marli grabbed the front of Sten's shirt as she darted backward into her room, kicking the door closed as soon as he was through it.

With no natural windows to this internal room, the only illumination came from a small desk lamp in the corner.

The interruption had replaced the distance between them. They stared at one another, waiting for the other to move or speak.

Just weeks ago, Marli had viewed this male as her mortal enemy. Forced time together had eroded that hard stance and she'd allowed the carnal aspects of her opinion of him to seep into the fissures.

Enemies no longer.

He'd offered a heartfelt apology that had truly hit home.

Even though she hadn't fully let him off the hook, she understood the motivation behind his previous actions.

He waited, gaze unwavering, expression calm, though his pulse ticked at his throat, his entire body taut.

Her fingers reached toward the buttons of his shirt and he sprang, dragging her against him.

Again, he stopped a breath from her lips. "Do you want this?"

With a quick intake of breath, she nodded.

"Do you want me?"

She blinked, nodding again.

"Say it, Marli and I'm yours. Only yours." He swallowed, the muscles in his throat tense.

Her eyes widened at those last two words. She licked her lips, seeking to comprehend his unexpected words. "Only mine?"

He pulled her reaching hand over his chest, where his heart thumped. "Only yours. But you have to say it. And only if you mean it."

She remained crushed against him. His desire hard against her heated core.

She searched his face for any underlying insincerity in his words, but detected none.

She swallowed. *He means it.*

"Unless you want this to be absolutely casual," he said, but the tension in his voice indicated that he preferred the former option.

She swallowed as his words registered deep into her subconscious. Words that whispered of a heart once broken. Asking her not to break it again if he gave it to her.

'Only yours. But you have to say it. And only if you mean it.'

She stared into his eyes, blinking as the words hit home.

So unexpected. So... *honest.*

His heart thumped under her palm.

I've had my heart broken too.

She thought he'd just want to get her into bed. Every male in the mountain probably did, just because she was one of the few females that was there and the only one that didn't have a mate.

Her free hand slid along his jaw, her thumb caressed the ridge of his lower lip, holding his gaze as she answered him. "I *do* want you. Very much. I just... I just don't know how long it will last..."

Because it never does...

He nodded, pressing his lips against the pad of her thumb. "It's enough to start."

"It's enough for now." She pulled his face closer so that she could finally press her lips to his.

She turned the hand pressing against his chest, so she could press his palm to her chest in turn.

It remained there for a long moment, warm and reassuring, until he splayed his fingers and slid them up along her throat to cradle her face the way she held his and deepened their kiss.

Marli had expected his mating to be intense—hurried.

Sten *was* intense in his attentions, but unhurried—intentional.

She groaned as his tongue swept her lip and opened to him, drawing him into her as her hips ground against his.

He pulled her fingers, twisting their hands so that they were behind her back as his other hand slid to her waist, then roamed lower to caress her ass.

Reaching down, she unbuckled her belt, then his. Unbuttoned her waistband, then his.

He unbuttoned his shirt, tugged it off, then pulled hers over her head.

Zippers followed; denim sagged at their hips as he continued to kiss her mouth. Her hands pushed until his jeans dropped to the floor, then backed away just enough to free herself too.

His gaze fell to her bright green lace panties.

Hers dropped to his throbbing erection.

He reached for her; she danced away.

Sliding her hands up behind her back, she unhooked her bra and slid it from her shoulders.

His gaze lingered on her breasts before returning to her face.

He reached for her again, pulling her against him.

She gasped as he slid between her thighs to pulse against the soaked lace.

He was hot and hard. She sizzled, wet, and so ready.

His lips met hers, then blazed a trail downward, only giving enough space between them to taste her nipples.

Savoring, teasing, nibbling. With a final suckle, he continued his worshipful path downward over her ribs and belly.

Breath quick and shallow, she watched as he pressed his face against the green lace and inhaled deeply before pressing kisses along her thighs.

On his knees, his fingers tugged at the lace, inching it down, pressing his lips where it had been before.

Her hands roamed his muscular shoulders and thick, silky hair as the heat of his mouth pressed to her mound.

The lace dropped below her knees to the floor.

Sten's hands slid up her thighs and gripped her ass as his tongue slid along her wet folds.

Her head fell back, eyes closed as she moaned his name.

His fingers slid into her, holding her in place as he feasted on her sensitive nub.

Sliding, teasing, pumping until she came.

He lapped up every drop of her and kissed his way back up her body as she clung to him on shaking legs. Her hand wrapped around his length, caressing and kneading him the way he'd tended her.

As she lowered herself, he stopped her. "Not this time."

Instead, he held her face as he claimed her lips. She tasted herself as his tongue swept hers. Her grip tightened as she stroked him.

He backed her to the nearest wall, lifting her knee over his hip.

She aligned his pulsing head to her sensitive center. With a single thrust, he slid home, shoving her back up against the wall.

They both groaned as he rested his forehead on her shoulder for just a moment. When he lifted his head, the desire writ across his features stole her breath away. His hooded gaze lingered on her mouth.

She claimed him, sliding her tongue into his mouth as he thrust into her again and again, increasing his speed and impact until she ascended again.

He stopped, filling her to his base, and released her mouth. One hand held her face, the other was planted against the wall.

He slid out to the tip, then inched back in again, and again, holding her gaze.

Every nuance in his expression, with every stroke, stoked the blaze within her. His passion mirrored her own.

She wanted him as much hard and fast as she wanted him slow and steady.

She just wanted him.

He struggled against closing his eyes as he neared his peak.

He filled her again.

She gripped him with her inner walls and bucked, inciting him to give in.

With her legs locked around his waist, she used her calves to press him into her harder and faster.

Staring into his beautiful eyes, she came again, sheathing, gripping, milking him to come with her.

He did, which rolled her into another wave of bliss.

Unwilling to relinquish him, she held him tight as he rested his forehead on her shoulder, her hands stroking his nape and scalp.

Once he had caught his breath, he lifted his face to hers, kissed her like she was fragile, then carried her to the bed, where they stayed until morning.

Chapter 16

The heavy dungeon door of the antechamber creaked open.

Clive squinted into the shadows beyond the prison bars where he and Merwin had been dumped and left to rot.

Stenlen?

He moved into the dim light toward their cell.

"What the fuck do you want now, traitor?" Clive snarled. "Don't you have some ass-kissing to do with that murderous usurper?"

Stenlen glanced at them, considering. He had an odd glint in his eyes that Clive had never seen before. Not on Sten.

Merwin approached, standing next to Clive, ready to hear what Sten had to say.

But Sten didn't speak. His hand flicked the thick dungeon keys around their iron ring.

Clive and Merwin exchanged uncertain glances.

Selecting a key, Sten inserted into the lock and give it a firm twist. It clicked, jerking open. He stepped back, allowing the door to drift further open.

"What is this, Sten?"

He tilted his head toward the wooden antechamber door.

"Isn't Mountainside afraid of what we'll do if we're loose?"

Sten shrugged.

Clive looked to Merwin again, whose eyes were glued to Sten.

"What's with him?" Clive murmured.

"Don't know, don't care. If he's letting us out, then we get the fuck out before he changes his mind."

"Do you think he's fucking with us?"

"Let's find out." Merwin pushed forward. "Whatever's going on has to be better than staying locked up in there indefinitely. Besides, there's two of us. We can take him."

Clive followed Merwin out. "Think so? This is Sten we're talking about here."

Merwin eyed their liberator, then followed his lead out of the antechamber. "Maybe."

Where the fuck are the guards?

He led them in the opposite direction from the steps that would lead up and out.

Instead, he guided them along several tunnels, each darker than the last, to a door tucked away in a corner of the dungeon, behind an abandoned store room.

He pulled a gold key from his pocket, muttered something, and unlocked this door.

It swung open, and cooler air hushed toward them.

The doorway was nothing but a black rectangle against the darkness of the underground room.

Sten stepped back, waiting for them to proceed.

Even with their acute dragon vision, they couldn't see much.

"Flashlight?" Merwin prompted.

He shook his head.

"Asshole," Clive muttered, following Merwin across the threshold.

He gulped, hoping there wasn't a mile-long drop ten feet in.

He didn't hear the door close. Just the click of the key turning in the lock.

"Fucker."

"Just keep going," Merwin growled. "Either we get out, or we die forgotten down here."

"Not fucking comforting, Merwin."

"Shut up, Clive. Walk or don't. I'm going."

At least their cell had been lit.

I fucking hate the dark.

And being alone.

Clive huffed, then followed the sounds of Merwin's feet, echoing off the close rock walls.

Chapter 17

Sten lay with his arm propped behind his head on the pillow.

Marli slept, curled over his side, her hair in wild disarray, tickling his chest and shoulder with every breath.

Reluctant to wake her, he carefully slid his other arm around so that he could gently brush the hair aside.

As much so that he could see her sleeping face as to relieve the tickle.

Something in him eased, but not in the way he'd expected.

In the beginning, Sten was sure that once he got her into bed—or wherever—the drive to have her would fade, like it always had in the past with other women, be they humans, other paranormals, or dragons.

He'd also expected her to indicate he should leave once she was done with him. That was also the norm with Aeleftherian dragonesses. Human women were often the opposite, but none of them held his interest for long. He wanted someone that would understand him; like another dragon.

Unable to help himself, his fingers trailed down her silky smooth skin, along her arm, around the bent elbow, toward her fingers splayed on his chest.

I can't believe I said that.

'Only yours. But you have to say it. And only if you mean it.'

And she hadn't laughed in his face or sent him away.

It hadn't occurred to him to offer her his heart. The words were out. Spoken from elsewhere. Uncontrolled. A piece of his youthful self had surfaced in that moment. Sten drew a deep breath, noting that he didn't regret it.

Deep in sleep, she was utterly vulnerable.

The contact of her warm body against his added to the odd wobbling sensation in his gut that threatened to work its way up into his chest.

He'd never allowed himself to relax into thoughts of this kind of contentment—not since his youth.

Too dangerous.

Marli had wriggled into some unknown crevice, poked the raw parts of him that should hurt like hell, but instead soothed him and his beast. She wasn't soft. Not gentle and nurturing in any obvious sense.

Once she got past the need to thrash him for being her enemy, she just gave him the space to *be*.

Another new revelation to him.

To just *be*.

Sensing the change in his body, Marli stirred. Her thick black lashes swept upward. Her golden gaze swept his face and smiled. She sighed, nuzzled her cheek against his chest, and planted a kiss over his heart. Her fingertips trailed over his skin and traced the tattoos across his chest. "What are these?"

"Emblems of different tribes I spent time with in my early days before Kargassa invited me to the mountain."

"You don't have one for the mountain?"

"No, I don't. Never thought to have one done."

"And this one?" Her finger traced along the name inked across his ribs.

He sucked in a breath.

Tell her or not?

His heart pounded. "My youngling."

Her head popped up to stare at him, eyebrows raised as she studied his face. "You don't want to talk about it?"

He shrugged. "There's nothing to talk about."

She frowned.

He finally blew out his breath, rubbing his thumb against his temple. "All I have is a name."

"Oh," she whispered, then lay her head back on his chest.

Dimly, he heard the elevator door chime. He tensed as the sound of feet rushing along the halls drew his attention to the door.

Marli sat up when Kymri's voice came through the door, followed by knocking. She frowned, leaving the bed to pull her clothes on.

Sten did the same, gathering his clothes to dress.

With a final glance to see that Sten was presentable, she opened the door several inches. "Kymri? What's wrong?"

She pushed the door open. "We have to talk. Clive and Merwin—"

"Clive and Merwin, what?" Sten stepped forward as he finished buttoning his shirt.

Kymri's eyes widened, glancing from Sten to Marli and back again. "They—I—they've disappeared." She snapped her lips closed.

"What? Where's Jori?"

"Looking for you," Kymri scowled, her gaze glued to Sten's face. "You'd both better come with me." She spun toward the door.

"What do you mean, they've disappeared? How do two imprisoned dragons disappear?" Marli demanded, catching up to Kymri's quick strides.

Kymri glanced over her shoulder at Sten as he followed them. She whispered to Marli, "How long has this been going on? You know what? Never mind, I don't need to know. Not really, anyway."

"Kymri, you're not making sense. And..." It was Marli's turn to glance over her shoulder at Sten, who simply kept walking as though he wasn't rushing along right behind them. "It's new."

"Okay, well..." she left off as she pushed the elevator button, casting Sten another glance, as though he too might disappear.

The elevator doors swished open. Jori looked up, expression tight as he glanced between the women. When his gaze landed on Sten. "Good, you found him."

Trepidation wormed through him.

Everyone stepped into the close space.

The hairs on Sten's nape prickled.

Eamerson joined them two floors up. He also stared at Sten with concern as he stepped in with them.

"Why the fuck does everyone keep looking at me like I've sprouted a second head?"

No one answered, or looked at him again, until they all stepped off, seeming to ensure he was still with them.

Marli caught his eyes and gave a little shrug.

The growing knot in his gut eased when she slipped her fingers between his.

Elora and a cluster of male dragons waited in the council room. Turning away from the view through the great windows, Sten recognized them as some of the mountain deputies that helped keep things under control, two of which were currently serving as prison guards.

"News?" Jori directed his question at them.

"Searches are being conducted all throughout the mountain, but none of the internal security cameras have picked them up."

"None?" Sten's brows went up.

"What do they cover?" Jori asked.

"All living and public spaces from the lowest elevator floor upwards. There aren't any below that, because those levels were magicked with Kargassa's security spells. That kind of magic interferes with the tech." Sten said.

"So Merwin and Clive are still in the lower levels somewhere?"

"We've searched every area we can access."

"Can access?" Jori's brow went up.

"Some tunnels were always off limits to everyone but Kargassa himself. We can't get into those without keys."

"And none were forced open or broken?"

The deputy shook his head. "The ones with simple locks are spelled to act like normal doors, but can't be broken or forced open, even with dragon strength."

Eamerson paced the length of the windows, one hand in his pocket while the other pinched his lip. "If there are secret exits, they'd be behind Kargassa's spelled doors. So either someone has a key, or whoever let them out is hiding them somewhere in the mountain, and also knows how to bypass the security cameras."

"Who would have a key?" Marli asked.

"Only Kargassa." Eamerson said.

"Who was the last to see Clive and Merwin?" Sten asked the deputies.

"You were." Craig said.

Sten blinked and jerked his head. "What? I haven't been down there in a few days." He looked from the deputies to Jori. "Not since I was there with you and Odson."

Jori studied Sten, as did Kymri and Elora. The deputies had already told them that.

The muscles in Sten's chest and gut shriveled inward. His gaze dropped to Marli's stony face.

He straightened his shoulder and spine, looking across the room to Eamerson, who also studied him as though he was working out a riddle. He nodded to Sten.

"You think I let them out?" Sten swiveled his gaze back to Jori.

His king.

Jori didn't answer him for a long moment as he weighed Sten's reaction, staring back, unapologetic, but the flicker of disappointment in his eyes couldn't be masked.

Sten had worked alongside his new king tirelessly to prove his trustworthiness, doing his duty to hold the mountain together. He'd envisioned the glimmer of what could be for this tribe in Jori during that time.

Stenlen had finally begun to hope that there actually could be peace between the tribes.

But at the first sign of trouble, the king and council turned to him with suspicion. The budding hope popped like a fragile soap bubble.

The deputy spoke up. "No one else went into the antechamber after you did last night. Not until Randal brought down their breakfast when they came in to relieve us from our shift."

"Last night?" Marli asked, confusion tightened her brow.

"Yes, last night." Craig frowned.

"That can't be right. You're sure?" she said.

The deputy sucked in a breath at her questioning, darted a glance at Jori, then Kymri, and carefully answered Marli. "Stenlen came by the antechamber, suggested we take a short break while he went into ask a few more questions. We unlocked the door for him, he went in and we took off for a few minutes as he suggested.

When we came back, the door was locked and he wasn't waiting around for us."

"We didn't think there was any reason to check in afterward." Randal shrugged.

"You're sure it wasn't someone else?" Marli tried again.

Neither deputy hid their annoyance as Craig answered. "Everyone in this tribe knows Sten. The king's man." He emphasized the last few words.

"Well, that doesn't make any sense," Marli planted her fists on her hips.

"Yeah, well, we didn't think so either. But here we are," he snarled back.

Marli stepped to within a couple of feet of him, looking up into his face and held his gaze, staring him down from below.

Sten suppressed a smile at her boldness.

"Sten couldn't have gone down to let those two idiots out of their cell last night, because I was with him all night. And I sure as hell didn't go down to the dungeon to let them out."

The shock of Marli's unapologetic assertion rippled through Sten, leaving his heart racing with relief.

"He was with you?" Jori's surprised voice pulled Marli's attention away from the deputy.

She turned toward him, "All night."

Jori nodded. "Good. That's sorted. Now we need to figure out what the fuck is going on, if some apparent duplicate of Sten managed to not just fool the deputies, but magically made our prisoners disappear, too." To

Eamerson, Jori said, "Review the camera footage around the elevators and stairwells for the time that Sten was supposed to have been bi-located."

Relief flooded through Sten, but he couldn't shake the sense of dread that he had even been suspected of betraying them.

Eamerson nodded, "Our tech team is already working on it." He hesitated.

"What is it?"

Eamerson pinched his lip again as he looked to the deputies before answering Jori. "There have been other issues among the tribe similar to this, where one male is adamant they saw someone doing something, while someone would also swear they were in another area of the mountain. But complaints of all kinds have risen since your ascension, sire—Jori."

"Hackles are up, the guys are edgy, and some are pushing the limits. We've been very busy the last while," Randal said, weary.

Elora stepped forward, "I've heard of this sort of thing happening before, but never encountered it myself."

"Encountered what?"

"Shape shifting. Morphing."

"Humor me here; I was ignorant of the paranormal world until a couple of months ago. You're telling me that people can shape shift into anyone? Not just into dragons or bears? But into other people?"

Elora replied, "They're extremely rare, Jori. It's more likely that if there is something beyond just edgy males with elevated testosterone, then it's spell work."

Jori pinched the bridge of his nose and drew in a deep breath as he looked at his mother. "Okay, so dopple-ganging is a thing."

"If it's spell work, then the magic user would need to access some genetic material from whomever they're duplicating."

"That's not difficult in a place like this. Just go to the aerie or training grounds." Revulsion rolled through Sten's gut at the idea that someone might have taken some piece of him in order to impersonate him. "But we don't know for sure that's what happening here."

"We're not discounting it, if it's a thing that exists. If Clive and Merwin are still in this mountain, we have to find and stop them before they endanger Aeleftheria." Jori said. "Eamerson, I want to go over those reports that you're concerned about. Sten, you should join the search patrols."

"I'll go too," Marli said.

Jori nodded. "Where are we on the communications tower replacement?"

"The steel beams to rebuild the tower haven't come in yet."

"Can you get a message out to Aeleftheria?" Jori turned to Marli.

"Our communication relays are slow, but yes, we can try," Marli said. "When we go out on patrol, I'll fly out to see if I can spot Red's ship. She's often just off the coast at this time of year. She'd get the message back more directly than the relay."

"Let's get to it." Jori nodded, dismissing everyone.

Chapter 18

Marli waited her turn on the hangar platform, opting go last as a precaution.

She ignored the males in favor of the mountain vista as, one by one, they stripped, shifted and launched.

"Ready?" Sten called to her just before he shifted into his dragon.

She turned in time to see the magic surround his muscular human flesh, shimmer and swirl, drawing out the ancient reptilian beast that occupied part of his soul.

His mass expanded, scales erupted, coating his skin to protect the bones and organs. Finally, his tail elongated and wings bloomed from his back.

It happened in a matter of seconds, but it still took her breath away.

One of her favorite things was watching other dragons transform into their more powerful selves. The process was the same, but each differed in their own unique ways.

She held onto the feeling of marvel a little longer, noting that the anxiety that had gripped her the last few times she'd watched him change was smaller now. It didn't fill every limb, as it had in the past, but just a spot at her nape warning that she couldn't let her guard down.

Not yet.

Sten glanced at her before taking one powerful step forward, launching off the edge of the stone platform that jutted from the mountainside hangar.

Her gaze followed him as he angled toward the stream of other males that were part of their search squad.

It'll be okay, Marli. They may be bigger, but you're faster.

On her previous outings, she had noted every crevice that would fit her body, the way the winds behaved around the peaks, and where the forested terrain rolled toward open ground until it hit civilization or ocean.

Alone in the hangar, she shed her clothing, drew a deep breath and let her dragoness free.

Tipping over the edge, her wings snapped out, pushing down to raise her body upward. She breathed a little deeper, filling her lungs with fresh air to scrub out the funk of the mountain.

Even if she couldn't see the other dragons, she'd be able to follow the stream of their scents. Marli ignored most of them, focusing on Sten's.

She flew lower than they did, navigating close enough to see between the trees below in case the prisoners were in human form on foot.

No humans. Just bounding deer, ambling bears, and all manner of scurrying creatures and birds. A pack of wolves eyed her warily, but maintained their course.

Once she ran out of mountain range, she ascended to Sten's height, signaling that she'd break off now. As soon as he acknowledged, she veered away, rolled, and continued her ascent.

Once over inhabited areas, she had to ensure she was high enough to be mistaken for a plane or a bird until she reached the coast.

As soon she spotted the glimmering ribbon of ocean in the distance, she breathed a little deeper.

Familiar. Home. Now to find Red out in this expanse.

Marli spotted the whale pods and adjusted her course.

Come on, come on, come on...

She blinked against the brilliance of the sun over the open water until she spotted the southern coast of Nova Scotia and adjusted again.

Her muscles cramped. Just as she started thinking about circling back to Seal Island to rest, a splotch of color on the horizon sent a thrill through her chest.

Yes!

Marli circled overhead, waiting for the signal flag that they saw her.

As soon as the flag went up, the rowboat lowered so that Red could meet her.

Marli descended, filling her lungs with air, happy to plunge into the ocean. Careful to pierce the surface at a perfect angle so as not to topple the ship with shock waves, she slid along the surface, snatching at a few fish here and there. As soon as the keel of Red's boat appeared, Marli shifted into her human form and broke the surface of the water.

"Hey Mar, I hear you're rolling through a shit storm these days." Red reached a hand out to help her climb into the boat.

"It's hitting everything, Red. Things might get a bit messy back home." Marli grabbed the terry robe from the bench beside her and pulled it on.

Red rolled her eyes. "When isn't it?"

"Two of the males that attacked us are on the loose again."

"Fuck." She eyed Marli. "You need me to alert them?"

"Yeah. Communications are off line at the mountain for a few days and I need to keep an eye on what's going on in that lair a little longer. Jori's definitely an ally, but changes of power are never smooth."

"Right," Red sighed, expression pained.

"Your day will come, Red. May as well accept it."

"I hate politics. If Jori wasn't the male king of our enemy, I *might* feel sorry for him. Being an heir sucks."

Marli shrugged. "Enjoy your freedom while it lasts, luv. Things are changing."

Red snorted but turned serious. "For real, huh?"

Marli nodded. "Regina is going to need you. Especially if those two males spread the word of Aeleftheria's location, which I'm sure they're bound to do."

"I'll go right away. I just need to alert my crew." Red's expression turned unusually somber. "Be careful in that mountain, Marli. Aeleftheria needs you."

Marli reached out to squeeze the errant princess' hand. "We need you too, Red. And Kymri misses you—you should see her with that little bump. The hormones are making her mushy!"

Red laughed. "I have to see that for myself. Mushy and Kymri are two words I could never have imagined in the same sentence."

Marli stood, slipped the robe off and lay it on the bench before jumping over the side of the little boat without a splash.

When she surfaced, she asked, "Red, have you heard of The Consortium?"

Red's brows lifted. "Unfortunately, yes. What's going on that *you* have?"

"I'm not sure. Odson is looking into something to do with them. As soon as he knows anything, we'll let the queen know."

"Right. Double alert. Give Kymri my love and be careful. All of you."

"I will. You too." Marli sank beneath the water, giving the rowboat plenty of clearance before shifting back into her dragon. She swam some distance before she breached the surface like a powerful orca, snapped her wings out and caught the air currents to ascend.

Banking, she pointed her nose back toward the mountain range.

Sten drew another breath, scenting.

Marli had been gone for hours longer than she estimated. Clive and Merwin had been Sten's wingmen for as long as they'd served as Kargassa's enforcers. They were capable trackers.

Had Merwin and Clive found her? Had one of the other guys gone after her?

He snarled.

Maybe she couldn't find her contact, or maybe she just decided to return to Aeleftheria.

Would she leave Kymri and Elora? She hadn't struck me as the type...

But then, she also had duties of her own to fulfill to her queen.

What the fuck are you thinking, Sten? Stop looking for her. Last night was... last night. Focus on finding those two idiots before they do irreparable damage.

A roar in the distance drew his attention. Tilting his wings, he turned toward the call. Moments later he joined several of the other searchers, circling over a group clustered on the ground around a rocky outcrop.

Finding a clear enough spot to land he shifted and jogged toward the gathered males. "What did you find?"

"Two sets of prints from this opening through the forest," Randal pointed through the trees opposite to where Sten had approached.

Another male came running toward them. "The prints turn dragon. They're long gone."

Fuck.

"Okay, what about this tunnel?"

"It goes back some distance, but seems to be a dead end. Either they were hiding in there, or they can walk through walls."

They can walk through walls if they're magicked.

Sten nodded. "You two report what you've found so far to Eamerson. You three go back in and search for any anomalies. The rest of you, continue searching both at the ground level and the sky. We might catch up to them."

"Why don't we just let them go?" Randal said. "Why are you walking free and they aren't?"

Sten spun at the challenge, walked up to Randal and looked him in the eye, tired of the same provocations. "They threatened the king's pregnant mate, and his mother, a political representative of a foreign nation."

"That was before he was king, Sten. Merwin and Clive were just following Kargassa's orders."

Sten clenched his jaw.

He'd repeated those same words to himself. He glanced at the other males around him. Many of them wore expression indicating they thought the same.

Before he could answer, a dragon roar echoed through the mountain range—and across his flesh. That wasn't the call of a male.

Marli.

Sten was running for the nearest clearing, heart hammering in his ears.

As soon as there was enough room between the thick pines, he shifted and launched, snapping branches as he went.

The fierce snarl resounded again, urging him on.

He was dimly aware that a few of the others trailed behind him. Sten sped through the mountain range, searching until he spotted three figures in a narrow valley. He drew a deep breath to control the crimson haze that crept around his vision when he registered the scene.

Purple claws confirmed Marli's identity.

Backed against a waterfall, two males nipped at her tail and wings, darting back when she snapped her jaws, taking chunks of flesh from their snouts or anywhere she could reach. She lashed out with a fore claw, swiping one aggressor's face while she swung her tail to collide with the other's.

Sten hit one of the males full force, bone and scale crunching against the jagged rock of the waterfall, then grabbed the other by the throat, whipping him against the other side of the valley.

Marli skittered backward, panting and growling.

The first male recovered, taking another snap at her.

Sten repositioned himself so that his body surrounded her. Facing her opponents, he snarled, daring them to try again.

Two of the males he'd overheard during the sparring session.

Not Clive and Merwin.

The other males hovered or circled nearby, observing. No one moved in to support him.

Sten looked up as several of the deputies that had been searching on foot also appeared overhead.

Goliath circled around, then landed next to Sten, snarling at the offenders, forcing them to back off.

Sten slammed the end of his barbed tail into the mountain beside him, causing the rock to crumble down into the river.

The two offenders took off.

No one stopped them, but no one followed them either.

Beneath him, Marli sagged, trembling against the ground, her claws still gripping the rock face.

She's exhausted.

Then he smelled blood. It was smeared along the cliff face where she'd been scraped along its face. Chunks of scale and flesh clung to the rock. Her wings were shredded in sections, which inhibited her ability to fly.

He lowered his body against hers so that his chest and throat rumbled along her shoulder and the back of her neck.

With a great sigh, she released her magic, transforming back into her human self, allowing Sten to support her in his fore claw. Cradling her close to his chest, he used his powerful hind legs to launch himself into the sky.

The others moved out of his way.

Goliath followed him back to the mountain.

Chapter 19

Confined to her quarters, Marli drifted in and out of sleep for several days while she recovered.

The investigation into Clive and Merwin's disappearance went on without her.

She ached from shoulder to knee on one side and she prayed she wouldn't scar from all the gashes and scrapes.

The mountain tribe didn't have an infirmary like the Aeleftherian citadel did, and she was going stir crazy, spending most of the time alone as her mind replayed the events in the valley.

Exhausted from so much flying, her energy lagged and she'd allowed her attention to drift.

Nearly back to the mountain range, she'd dropped her guard, letting her thoughts drift to Stenlen.

He'd offered her his precious self.

She couldn't take it.

Marli needed time to examine what was in her own heart. And when she'd awakened that morning to look up into his face, everything clicked into place in that moment.

And then another revelation.

He has a youngling that he knows nothing about.

Her heart twisted. She wanted to know about him. About his past. They really weren't enemies anymore. He'd been courteous and attentive. His love making... she blew out a breath.

Otherworldly.

She smiled, until her mind returned to the valley.

Out of nowhere, a male body-slammed her into the mountain above the waterfall, dragging her along its rock face, shredding her wing and scales so that she couldn't fly.

The other moved in.

Her heart hammered in her chest at the memory. She squeezed her eyes shut to block out the fear and rage and helplessness she'd felt. She'd never been so vulnerable in her life.

And then Stenlen was there, and that was all that mattered.

She sobbed, covering her face with her hands, even though she was alone in the room.

He came. He got her out and wouldn't let her go except to pass her to his big friend so that he could shift down to his human form.

Sten carried her to her bed, lay her down with more gentleness than she'd experienced since she was a child, and stayed all night by her side as she dipped in and out of consciousness while her magic worked furiously to repair the damage.

Her head ached and her body throbbed from shoulder to knee.

Stenlen Flintail had saved her life, because she would have fought to the death to prevent....

She drew a deep, steadying breath to ease her pounding heart.

It didn't happen. He was there.

With her emotions back under control, she stared across the room at the closed door, determined to block thoughts of the attack. She wouldn't let it overrun her.

It's done. He was there.

Her eyes sagged, but not wanting to sleep anymore, she powered her phone on to play a merge and match game to bide the time and redirect her mind.

Her phone pinged.

The communications tower is back up?

Her thumb swiped the screen, scrolling through missed messages and emails.

Kolina Steelscale, Kymri's mother, had left Aeleftheria for the continent, searching for Kymri, demanding to know the mountain's location to bring her home.

A knock drew her attention. Kymri eased the door open and poked her head through the gap. "Good, you're awake."

Marli held up her phone. "Your mom's on the rampage."

Kymri sighed, settling on the bed next to Marli. "You didn't read all the messages?"

Marli scrolled through the rest, heart racing, sitting up straight. "Clive and Merwin. Those assholes attacked the island again? So they *did* escape the mountain."

"The queen sent my mother to Black River to search for us."

"Oh no. I was too late. Red must not have got the message to them in time."

"I don't know about that, but Jori and I are going to take the plane with Elora and Jonathan to meet up with her and Odson. They're tracking Merwin and Clive along the coast. Apparently, they're recruiting."

Kymri stopped Marli from trying to get out of bed. "You need to rest"

"I need to go."

"I need you here, Marli. Jori is leaving Sten and Eamerson in charge. I need you here for me and Elora. I don't want to you leave you like this, but it's important."

"Why, what's going on?"

"Your attack isn't going over well with a lot of the males. Sten's been run off his feet stamping out arguments and stopping fights before things escalate."

Marli sagged back against the headboard, drawing a slow, steady breath.

When she looked at Kymri, there were tears in her eyes. "I don't know what I would have done if he hadn't intervened."

They both knew it was a lie.

Marli would have fought like hell no matter what, but in the end, it would have been a losing battle.

Kymri squeezed Marli's hand. "He and Goliath have been taking turns guarding your door. The whole corridor is off limits.

"Guarding my door? Goliath? The big guy?"

Kymri nodded toward the door. "He's out there now."

"I should thank him." Marli studied Kymri's face, her expression somber. "You should have let me tell Aeleftheria that Clive and Merwin were a problem as soon as I got here."

Kymri stiffened. "We couldn't have predicted that they would escape."

"There's too much turmoil in this mountain to honestly believe that it wasn't a possibility."

Kymri sighed, dropping her head into her hands. "It's like a fucking powder keg in here. There's too much resentment about how things happened."

"We should go back. When you meet up with Kolina, go back with her. We can do more good by shoring up our defenses."

"I don't believe that."

"I know you don't. But you can't change centuries of ingrained beliefs overnight."

"Not overnight. Jori's got a strong foothold. This is it, Marli. If Jori can't do this, it'll never happen."

"Just be careful out there, Kym. I still really don't think you should go. Especially if they're recruiting." Marli swallowed. "And I should be with you."

Kymri grabbed Marli's hand. "Don't worry, Elora's working her magic and calling on old friends. We'll be fine. I'm more worried about dealing with my mother than anything else out there right now."

Marli squeezed her hand back.

Kymri stood to leave.

Marli pulled the blanket back and eased her feet over the side, swatting Kymri's hand away. "I'm not so injured that I need a pregnant woman to help me up."

Kymri shrugged and stepped aside. "You should rest more." She reached for the neatly folded t-shirt and sweats stacked on the dresser, handing them to Marli.

"You sound like *my* mother." She grumbled as she pulled the clothing on.

Kymri snorted and rolled her eyes. "Better than mine. She'd have gotten you out of bed yesterday and told you to get back to your duties."

Marli laughed until pain streaked up her side, stealing her breath away. Her shoulder and hip throbbed in time with her heartbeat. Swaying on her feet, she held up her hand and resigned to move more carefully, making her way to the door. "Don't say it."

When she opened the door, her eyes landed on the big guy leaning against the opposite wall, arms over his chest and legs crossed at the ankles. He was so tall, the shock of red hair nearly brushed the ceiling when he straightened to his full height. She met his blue gaze.

"Good morning."

Even his greeting was a grumble.

She nodded. "Thank you for helping me get out of that... jam."

He nodded back. "You shouldn't be here."

His words struck her chest, and she sucked in a breath.

"None of you should be. But you are, and that shouldn't have happened. That sort of thing should never happen, so I understand now why you are. Here."

Marli blinked at him. She turned to Kymri, who moved into the door frame beside her.

"We all appreciated it, Frederick," Kymri said to Goliath.

His complexion gained a rosy hue.

The elevator doors swished open, drawing their attention to Stenlen striding toward them, eyes on Marli.

"She's awake," Goliath said.

"So I see."

"I'll let the others know she'll live."

Sten gave Goliath a nod as he left, without another word to Marli or Kymri.

"Hold the doors, Frederick," Kymri called out. "We'll just be gone a few days," she said to Marli and Sten, then left them alone in the hall.

Kymri's footsteps disappeared, the doors swished closed, and the only sounds were those of Sten and Marli's breathing in the otherwise vacant hall.

She looked up into his taut face as he hovered over her.

"How do you feel?"

She gave a short laugh.

He nodded.

Her gaze swept his tense body, over his broad shoulders and arms held out as though ready for something.

"Thank you," she met his eyes.

He sucked in a breath. "I'm sorry I didn't stop them from hurting you."

"You stopped them."

His fingers twitched.

She reached for his hand, recalling the relief she'd felt when his dragon body had enveloped hers.

Never in her life would she have imagined a male protecting her like that. Nor could she have admitted to herself that she welcomed it.

His arms around her, protecting her when she was most vulnerable. His tender hands and gentle lips as he kissed her forehead, his fingers that fluttered over her face when he brought her injured body into her room.

She turned his hand over in hers, and her other hand caressed this palm, causing his fingers to curl over hers.

"I'm glad you're okay." His voice was tight.

"Me too," she smiled.

The tension eased out of his shoulders.

She tugged his fingers as she backed into her room.

He stepped in, closing the door behind him with a soft click. His free hand slipped along her jaw and cheek.

She closed her eyes, pressing her face into the warmth of his palm with a sigh.

"Marli—" his lips remained parted, though no more words came. His eyes said it all.

For the second time, she blinked back tears. Closing them, she pressed her lips to his. She released his hand, entwining her arms around his neck.

He pulled her close.

She gasped as pain clawed through her.

His hand snapped away from her as though she'd shocked him.

Reaching for his hand, she pulled it close and placed it where it didn't hurt.

Ever gentle, his fingers splayed across her lower back while his other hand slipped along her nape to support her head as his kisses deepened.

His lips lingered before he finally broke away, dipping his head to the crook of her shoulder, arms wrapped around her so that she was completely enveloped in their safety and warmth.

He inhaled, releasing it with a long sigh.

She relaxed into him, laying her head on his shoulder.

"I guess we have work to do."

He nodded against her shoulder, then lifted his head, holding her gaze. "You okay to do this?"

Her hand found his again and squeezed. "I am."

Chapter 20

The investigation into Clive and Merwin's escape continued after Jori's departure, along with Kymri, Elora, and their human, Jonathan.

Sten was on duty outside Marli's room, ensuring no one bothered her while she slept. Phone gripped in hand, he inspected the stills Eamerson sent him from the security cameras.

He was frustrated to no end that they couldn't find whomever had let the prisoners out. Especially when he was the only suspect.

He'd reviewed the camera footage with Eamerson's tech crew, which clearly showed him emerging from the library toward the stairwell that led down. Then, half an hour later, he emerged from the stairs and took the elevator up to his floor back to his room. Many other males came and went during those time frames. The cameras only covered the elevator and stairwells, but he'd seen himself accessing floors and rooms he didn't normally frequent.

Eamerson also pointed out anomalies among other males, seeming to be in two places at once, which matched some of the complaint files he managed.

Since the escape, every male in the mountain was interviewed. Since the attack on Marli in the valley, more males volunteered to help with the investigation.

The culprits hadn't returned. They knew they'd sealed their fates when they'd risked going after her. No one pursued them either.

Unless they met up with Clive and Merwin, they weren't a threat to Aeleftheria—at least not immediately. And imprisoning them wouldn't help if the individual that freed the previous prisoners wasn't found. They could just let them out, too.

Or maybe that's what was needed? A way to entrap the mystery person...

He'd begun thinking along those lines when Goliath stepped out of the elevator and approached him to take his post outside of Marli's room.

The morning after Marli was confined to her room, Goliath had joined Sten in the hall without a word.

He hadn't explained himself, but it was clear he'd become Marli's personal bodyguard and Sten's strongest new ally in the mountain conflicts.

Hours later, he broke the silence. "It's good that our new king is planning a funeral for our old king. I want to be part of it."

The sincerity in Goliath's face prompted Sten to nod. "Come with me when I meet with Jori."

"Appreciate it."

The silence returned until Eamerson appeared to relieve Sten, and was equally surprised to see Goliath.

"I'm glad you joined the deputies, Frederick. Your work is really helping the tribe." Eamerson said to the larger man.

Goliath grunted.

"You're sure you have the time to do this?" Sten said to Eamerson.

"Jori requested it. There aren't many other males that he trusts enough yet. Besides, I can use the break from running around the mountain to do some administrative work." Eamerson pulled his tablet from the satchel he had slung across his chest. Setting it aside, he held up Kargassa's memoir. "And when I get through that, I have some light reading to entertain myself."

"No further leads?"

Eamerson shook his head. "If we rely solely on the footage, you're the only suspect. But Marli vouched for your whereabouts."

Goliath frowned at them. "What happened?"

Eamerson glanced from the big guy to Sten, who nodded for him to explain the situation.

"That doesn't make sense. If Sten was going to let them out, he'd have done it at the beginning, when everyone would have supported him to lead this tribe. Not now."

Eamerson raised a brow at Sten.

Sten scratched his forehead with his thumb. "Right, so we're exploring options to understand who else that could be and why."

Eamerson said, "I don't know anyone else that resembles Sten that could pass as him."

"Let me see the video." Goliath curled his fingers, prompting Eamerson to show him on his tablet.

Goliath squinted at the screen as he watched the clips. "Yep, that looks like you, but you're coming from the library. I've never seen you in the library, Sten."

"I've been there a couple of times," Sten crossed his arms.

"That day?" It was Goliath's turn to lift a brow.

"No, both times I went, I was with Marli."

"If that's not you, then this whole thing is creepy. And I don't know anyone that can pass as you either."

Sten grunted.

Goliath was quiet for a moment. "What other options are you thinking of?"

"Magic?" Eamerson offered.

Goliath laughed, looking between Eamerson and Sten. "You're kidding."

Sten shrugged. "Not unless you know of any shifters in this mountain that have the ability to borrow faces?"

"They aren't real."

Eamerson's brows lifted as he raised a finger. "According to the humans, we aren't real either."

"Okay, well, this conversation just got real weird. Sten, make sure you tell Jori about me and the funeral. I know some of the other guys would want in on that, too."

"I will. And thanks for helping in the search for the prisoners. Get some rest. I'll be back in a few hours." Sten said to Eamerson before making his way to the elevator with Goliath.

In the elevator, Goliath said, "You're not kidding about the magic idea."

"Nope."

"Creepy."

"Yep."

Chapter 21

Another long day over, Marli lay in her bed, enveloped in Sten's powerful arms.

She and Sten and Eamerson were still in charge of the mountain lair.

The funeral planning was nearly complete.

There were no further leads on whoever had freed Clive and Merwin.

There were still bickering males posturing throughout the mountain, though some of the reported instances seemed like petty disturbances being blown out of proportion.

Each night, Marli took Sten's hand, inviting him into her room. They hadn't mated since the night before Clive and Merwin's escape, but they had shared her bed since the morning she'd awakened to find Sten and Goliath guarding her door. They just kissed and talked and slept.

She learned a lot about Sten and his mountain; from the things he shared, and also in the subjects he hedged.

Though her magic was doing its best to heal the injuries, her movements were still ginger.

His touch was always tender.

Every time he brushed the hair away from her face, his fingers would caress the strands, marveling at their silkiness. She'd close her eyes and revel in the sensations he elicited. Goosebumps would rise on her skin and he'd smooth them out with his warm hands.

Marli sighed, cradling his arm. These last few days were a waking dream; scenarios she might have seen in a movie at Black River's little cinema. This simply wasn't reality in her world. Male and female dragons weren't tender. They didn't linger. They didn't snuggle.

Is this what it's like for Kymri and Jori?

For Elora and Jonathan?

None of the other Aeleftherians ever hinted at this sort of softness to their mating experiences.

It was always a thing to be done—enjoyed, yes—but not... this.

Whatever this was. She had no name for it.

And Sten? Her former enemy, her personal rogue turned tender lover.

Not like the human males she'd taken to her bed in past years, or other shifters, or even occasional dragons.

He was... different.

"What are we going to do?" Her whisper was loud in the silence of the room.

His lips slid along the shell of her ear. "I don't know." He pulled her so that her back pressed to his chest. "What do you want to do?"

Her breath caught. "No one's asked me that before."

"Duty." He sighed, lightly resting his chin on her crown.

She nodded against his chin.

Their phones vibrated.

Marli reached for hers on the table beside the bed as Sten pulled his from his pocket.

"They're coming back."

Marli groaned, "Thank *dragongoddess*, I hate being in charge."

Sten chuckled. The sound rumbled through his chest against her back.

She leaned into him again.

After a long moment, she said, "I have a feeling things are going to be different when they return."

"I think so, too."

"This might be the end of our time, Sten. I can't stay here."

"I know." His voice was a breath over her ear.

She shivered, closing her eyes, reveling in the feel of his body pressed to hers.

I don't want this to end.

She swallowed. "I want you, Sten."

He didn't answer.

"Sten?"

"You're still healing."

It wasn't what she meant, not entirely, but she would go with that because her chest ached too much to continue along the other thread. The real meaning behind her words.

She slid her fingers between his, guiding his hand over her breast as she pressed her bottom back into his groin.

Releasing his hand she reached around to the front of his pants. Seeking, she slipped her fingers behind the belt and waist band along his taut belly. The instant she touched his warm flesh, he hardened.

Sten groaned against her ear. "Marli."

She stroked him.

He kneaded her breast, rolling her nipple between his fingertips as his other hand cradled her face, turning her so that he could explore her lips.

Soon he released her breast and slid his hand into her panties, making her gasp against his mouth.

Desire shuddered through her.

"I need you inside me. Now." She bit his lip, then swept his tongue with hers.

Sten's hands left her so that he could unbuckle his belt and push his jeans down.

Marli tilted her hips back, seeking.

His warm fingers grazed her hip. "You're sure?"

She growled at him, pressing his hands so that they pushed the waistband of her panties down so that her bottom was bared to him.

Still, he didn't oblige.

He kneaded her hip and the soft flesh of her ass, eventually moving so that his hard length slid along her folds to rest on her nub.

She bucked, biting her lip as her juices coated him. His flesh scalded her.

She clenched her thighs together, holding him tight to her.

Marli pulsed; Sten throbbed.

The only sounds were those of their soft gasps and the whisper of the sheets below them as they lay on their sides, lost in the sensations they created for one another.

He slid back and forth, fanning her fire.

"Sten, come into me. Now."

"Marli—"

"*Now.*"

His hands slid around her waist, still careful not to aggravate the healing wound along her shoulder, hip, and thigh.

One hand across her pelvis, the other gripped her uninjured shoulder. He nuzzled her neck, teeth grazing a trail from below her ear down to her shoulder.

He growled as he tilted his hips and thrust, filling her to his base.

She cried out, "Yes! More."

Sten slid out, slamming home again, striking her sweet spot so that she quivered.

"Faster."

He obliged; harder, faster, growling.

It wasn't enough. She needed him to pound her into oblivion.

To forget.

She needed to forget all that she was and all that he was.

To forget for a little while that they would go back to their duties.

There was only here and right now.

Right fucking now.

"Fucking harder, Sten. Harder."

He pumped until he lost control.

"Marli..." he growled, right before he bit her shoulder in the traditional dragon mating way. "Mine."

The word reverberated through her. Pain enveloped her. The primal knowledge of a claiming ripped through her, making her come with an explosive growl of her own, gripping him with everything that she was.

Marli's dragon rose to the surface, reaching for Sten's. Seeking.

His magic flowed into her, taking hers into him when it withdrew on a gasp. It flowed back and forth, tangling, weaving, merging.

Her body shook, taking him again and again as he found his peak, surging into her shaking body again and again.

She hadn't meant for it to happen, but the drive to have him so deep inside of her triggered the instinctual need to claim and be claimed.

Sweat slicked their bodies. Their flesh tightened against the chill as they cooled, gasping to catch their breath.

Sten remained within Marli.

He didn't withdraw from her.

She didn't release him.

I can't. I can't let him go.

"Marli, I—"

Not yet.

She gripped him tight, still deep within her, and rolled her hips.

His breath shuddered against her nape.

Their magics flowed back and forth, his boosting hers so that the discomfort in her wounded shoulder, hip and thigh subsided.

She pumped him within her sensitive channel, ensuring he was as hard as he had been moments before.

Easing off of his tip, she turned around on her knees, pulling him up so that he met her lips.

She pulled the rest of her clothes off, then helped him out of his, letting them fall haphazardly around them.

Her arms encircled his broad shoulders. He dipped his head to taste her breasts, his tongue laving one, then the other. She gently pushed him back against the headboard, straddling his hips.

With firm hands encircling her waist, he leaned forward, kissing and licking her belly. His hands slid up her back. She reveled in the feel of his arms around her as she settled down to reclaim him.

... *to claim him.*

Aligned with his tip, she took him in, filling and expanding her sensitive channel with a soft gasp.

He throbbed against her sweet spot, making her moan.

When she caught her breath, she caressed his jaw and urged him to look into her face.

"I didn't mean for this to happen either, Sten. But it is."

She really hadn't.

His gaze flicked to the bite mark that stung her previously uninjured shoulder. He'd initiated the bonding. An ancient rite, through a moment of instinct.

For some, the bond happens without the rites—a spontaneous act of fate driven by their most primal selves.

For others, it's a conscious choice.

It seemed that for them, that it was a bit of both.

He reached for her face, his beautiful grey eyes fluttering over her features. "I didn't mean for it, either, but I don't regret it. I told you that I'm yours."

She nodded between his palms, understanding it deeply now. Her dragon rose to the surface within her again.

Claim him.

She clenched him deep within her as she watched the desire change his features.

Still, she hesitated.

What happens if I do? Everything is so frikking complicated.

His growl rumbled through his chest, making his entire body vibrate, and hers too.

She closed her eyes, bracing her hands on his shoulders, writhing atop him, allowing her body to hush her mind.

Her breath came fast as she ascended again. Opening her eyes, she looked down into his taut face, watching her with parted lips.

Holding his steady gaze, she moved faster.

"You're so beautiful," he breathed. His brow furrowed as his arms enveloped her waist, supporting her movement.

The contact of his hands up her back made her shiver, spiking her climb. She swallowed a moan, nearly there.

Ensuring her gaze was locked on his, he tilted his head, baring the sensitive flesh where his neck and shoulder met.

Claim him.

Heart hammering in her chest, fear and desire and the intense need to complete the claiming ricocheted through her.

Her dragon made the decision for her.

Magic rippled, heightening the sexual desire so that the instinct took over until she had no choice but to seek relief, and bit down on his shoulder. Dragon teeth descended just enough to puncture his skin. She tasted his blood. The flood of her magic into him dragged her up toward climax and when it surged back within her, in a tsunami of his magic twisted with hers, she crashed so hard her fingernails bit into his shoulders. He filled her as they rolled through wave after wave, magic, limbs, blood, sweat and mating fluids entwined.

Marli disengaged her teeth from his shoulder, spreading little kisses along the puncture marks.

Sten's arms tightened around her.

"Everything's going to be different." She whispered against his warm skin.

"It already is."

Chapter 22

Sam Egan glanced toward the library's main door before he grabbed a stack of books from the front counter, carried them to the back of the room, and deposited them on the desk for processing. With one last quick glance at the door, Sam descended the spiral metal stairs to the archives, continuing on from the first lower level down to the second and finally third, where almost no one else ever went. There'd been exactly seven interested visitors to this level in the last few decades. And that had been more out of a sense of curiosity about discovering that the archives existed than out of a need for serious research.

Sam moved toward the small workroom at the back of the lowest archival level, where the most important research and work happened.

The liquid in the prepared vial was almost clear enough for the next step. However, time was an issue now. This would affect the quality of the sample, but that couldn't be helped. Sam selected a few sap-covered scales scavenged from the forest during a routine walk and dropped them into the nearby mortar and pestle. A few even appeared to have bits of dried blood. All the better.

Since the scales were unusually dense, it took much longer to grind than most other samples. Hands at work, mind reciting the catalog of required steps, Sam hummed through the mixing. The wizard's recipe was tedious, but much better than the alternative.

Spells weren't absolutely necessary. The intricate details of the change could be done without them, but that way was barbarous and revolting. The natural way meant cannibalizing, which had been done once and only once, at the Master's request. The Master had wanted to see Sam's true ability for himself. Never again, he'd sworn, unless absolutely necessary for survival. Thankfully, the Master had agreed that the natural way was disgusting and had ordered the wizard to provide recipes that would work nicely, without that kind of indigestion. This was also much more precise, efficient, and discreet.

I'm so close to completing my mission.

Sam's hands tightened on the mortar and pestle, disrupting the flow, and nearly spilling the precious contents on the worktable.

Damnation.

Eyes closed, one breath drawn, the mixing resumed.

The key Sam had stolen during Kargassa's fateful initiation ceremony had granted access to most of the secret tunnels. Two had proved to be escape routes out of the mountain.

I still haven't found the god-forsaken vaults! They have to be in Kargassa's private quarters.

But there hadn't been sufficient time to locate them, during the brief excursions into that area of the mountain, and it was too risky to linger.

I have to try again.

The cell on the table lit up. The Master was growing impatient.

I can't afford to anger him. Not with Ani's life in his hands.

The bounty for this mission was far too high for failure.

Freedom for Ani. And prestige for Sam, who would join the Founders of the new era.

Which all depended on Sam's success.

Time to set aside the ground up sample, and collect the rest of the equipment required to measure and transfer it in proper quantities.

Done. Next, shake the vial to ensure complete dissolution.

It changed color, from chalky powder to brilliant green, then it faded to blue and reverted to white. Once it had settled into a thicker, grey substance, it was ready.

Sam tipped back the vial, grimaced against the foul taste, and swallowed.

Gasping and gagging, they checked their newly acquired pocket watch, keeping time.

Each experiment had completed faster than the last, and with less discomfort.

After recording the time, Sam grabbed the cell phone, set the digital timer, and hurried back up the spiral stairs.

"Hallo?"

Sam froze, ducking down below floor level to remain unseen.

"Anyone here?"

Frederick.

A regular patron. But it wasn't his usual day to exchange books.

Listening, breath held.

Frederick shuffled toward the back of the library. The sounds of books sliding and dropping on the desk resounded down the stairwell.

"Magic books? Who would look at those?" Frederick mumbled. "Creepy."

He sighed, moving around the back room where patrons weren't welcome.

Teeth clenched, tongue held, Sam waited.

"Where is he? There's nothing good left to read," Frederick grumbled, rummaging through other piles and shelves.

Frederick appeared in Sam's line of sight, looking through the overstock shelves.

Sam's annoyance prickled at the invasion of the off-limits room.

Go away!

The phone timer ticked down. This particular sample could not go to waste. Confirmation of the viability of this experiment was imperative.

"... come back later, I guess."

Sam sighed, eyes rolling, waiting for Frederick to leave the library.

As soon as the main door clicked shut, Sam darted out of hiding and sprinted forward.

Easing the door open, they confirmed that Frederick was gone.

In the elevator, sweat slicked Sam's hands, fingers drumming on a thigh, praying there wouldn't be any unfortunate encounters during the elevator ride.

Heart tripping, the doors opened and Sam strode as naturally as possible toward Kargassa's private rooms.

The rooms through the black doors had been turned into council chambers.

Ignore those.

The new king was away, but that didn't mean someone else wasn't around that could cause trouble. Using the spelled key, Sam slipped into the royal suite, gaze darting over every surface and possible hiding place.

Everything was constructed of marble or granite.

Breathe. Think. Where would Kargassa hide a vault? Would he bother to hide a vault?

The timer continued to descend.

Some humans installed safe rooms in their closets. Maybe Kargassa would do something similar.

The closet was almost as big as Sam's living space, full of expensive cashmeres, pristine leather shoes and belts, cuff links in every gemstone, to adorn any of the many tailored suits.

Beyond all of that was a wall of floor-to-ceiling mirrors, held in place with gold dragon claw brackets.

It has to be one of these brackets...

Key inserted, one twist caused a mirrored panel to pop outward and slide aside to reveal another chamber. It too was marble lined, as the bedroom and corridors had been. Conversely, this room was small and empty, except for a gold emblem fixed to the back wall.

There were no holes suitable for the key. Instead, there were five holes surrounding the carved dragon head.

On closer inspection, Sam determined they were meant for dragon claws.

Would it work?

Sam held up a hand, shifting it so that the fingers extended into claws.

The claws trembled as they dipped into the mechanism. Sharp needles punctured the soft flesh of the first joints.

Jerking back, blood dripped in little splats onto the white marble floor.

Sam scrambled to clean up the evidence while monitoring the emblem for activity.

Nothing. Damnation.

Blood oozed out of the claw slots, prompting more frantic wiping.

Time to go. Quickly. Steady.

Sam backtracked, locked the mirror back in place, hurried through the room, then into the corridor and back to the elevator at a normal pace.

Footsteps echoed down the hall.

Damnation!

The elevator doors opened. The phone's timer went off, the sound bouncing off of the marble walls.

A female dragon rounded the corner. She paused, looking at Sam.

The Aeleftherian.

"Jori?"

Sam stepped into the elevator, jabbing the button to close the door, and descended back to the safety of the library.

Staring at the reflection of the metal walls, Sam's appearance transformed from the long-haired, tattooed new king back to their own unremarkable features, clean skin and common hair style.

Sam shoved their hands into their pockets to hide the blood as much as to still the trembling.

Failed. Again. Damnation. I'm going to have to scavenge for more samples after I finish the Master's diary entry.

Every experiment needed to be recorded. Precisely.

Chapter 23

———✦✦·······✦✦———

"Jori?" Marli stepped toward the elevator, but it closed in her face. "Damn. Why didn't he say anything?" She muttered, resuming her course toward the council room. "Hey, why didn't you tell me everyone was back already?"

Sten looked up from Eamerson's tablet. "They're not."

"They should arrive in a few hours," Eamerson added.

"I just saw Jori go into the elevator."

"Just now?" The males exchanged glances.

"Yes, just now." Marli said, rolling her eyes.

Eamerson whipped his cell from his pocket, punching the call button. "Watch the surveillance cameras on the elevator right now. Then check back over the last thirty minutes." He glanced at Marli. "Use Ms. Fleetwing as a marker with the most recent timestamp to track King Mountainside's movements. No, he hasn't returned yet. Yes, that's bad. Mobilize the deputies and call me back."

As soon as Eamerson finished the call, he followed Sten out of the council room toward the elevator, nose twitching.

"I smell blood." Sten called the elevator up and inspected the buttons. "There's a blood smear here," he pointed at the panel.

"I have a droplet here," Eamerson said from beside the door to the royal suite. He touched it, then held his fingertip under his nose. "Smells like Jori, but it's not quite right. I also detect a hint of pine. I've cleaned enough his wounds after failed landings that I know the smell of it."

The door wasn't quite closed. Sten shoved the door open.

"We shouldn't go into the king's private quarters—" Eamerson said on impulse.

"He won't mind in this case," Sten countered, gaze glued to the floor.

Marli followed both males, scanning the room as they went, spreading out through the suite. "What was he doing?"

"Pretty sure that wasn't Jori, so I'd say it's a safe guess the imposter is after something of value."

"So we do have a thief on the loose in the mountain."

"I don't see any jewellery boxes or safes. Just clothes." Marli moved through the closet.

"Vault." Eamerson said. "They'd be after the vault."

"There's another blood smear under the mirror here," she called out.

Eamerson joined her at the back wall, locating the stain and within moments discovered the hidden keyhole in the bracket. He sucked in his breath.

"What did you find?" Sten asked from the door.

"The stain is smeared from under the mirror, where there's a keyhole."

"Shit." He strode forward to inspect it for himself.

"Do you think it's the same key that opens the tunnels?" Marli asked. "That this is the same person that freed Clive and Merwin?"

"And can somehow look like Jori, now." Sten ran a hand through his hair.

"It's possible they've done this before. We just wouldn't know."

"Not without asking Jori to confirm every instance of his appearance on the surveillance footage."

Marli's heart hammered in her chest. "If this person can pose as Jori, they have the power to incite the tribe to invade Aeleftheria."

"No one knows where it is, except me, Clive, and Merwin."

"They may have told him as payment for their freedom."

"Even if an invasion is their end goal, they were searching for something first." Sten said, rubbing his temple with his thumb.

"Jori wasn't carrying anything that I could see. So if they got what they came for, it's something small."

Eamerson pinched his lip in thought. "Do you think it could have something to do with why King Kargassa didn't invade right away?"

Sten sighed, "Who knows?"

"What if they're trying to get close to Elora or Kymri?" Marli scrubbed her hands over her face and back through her hair. "I have to consider they could be this imposter's target. Maybe they're in league with those males that went after me?"

Eamerson's phone chimed. "Yes? From the Library? Meet us there, but don't go in."

Sten was already headed back to the elevator with Marli and Eamerson close behind. There was another smudge of blood on the button for the lowest floor.

Goliath and a handful of deputies met them outside of the library's solid main door. There weren't any more visible blood stains to confirm the imposter had gone this way.

"I was just here. The librarian wasn't around."

"The footage didn't show Jori getting off the elevator at any point. We tracked four other males who got on and off the elevator since your call. Only one didn't register an entry."

Sten reached out to open the door.

Marli stopped him. "Let me."

Sten met her eyes. "If you're right about Aeleftherians being a target, then you can't risk going in alone. Especially so soon after the last attack."

"Or she could be wrong and none of these events are related," Eamerson said. "If that's the case, she might not be seen as a threat and could be an optimal distraction for us to go in unnoticed."

Sten's gaze flicked between them and to the waiting deputies. "Check every other room on this floor. Keep an eye out for any evidence of blood."

Goliath leaned close to Sten to whisper. "What if the creepy magic user is one of us?"

Marli considered this. Before Sten could answer, she strode toward the waiting deputies, hand extended. "I want to thank each of you for the work you've done here to help us enforce King Mountainside's efforts to maintain peace in the mountain during his absence."

Some registered confusion at her unexpected words, a few seemed pleased by the praise. They all extended their hands for her to shake. None had blood or fresh wounds on their hands that she could detect or smell.

"We good?" Sten asked.

"We're good," Marli nodded to Goliath with a pat on his expansive bicep.

The deputies departed to fulfill their duty.

"That was a very astute point," Eamerson said, keeping his voice low in the corridor.

"It is, and one we should keep in mind. This imposter has impersonated Sten, and now Jori. We don't know who else, or how long, this has been going on. They really could be anyone at any time."

"Or why; so be careful," Sten said to Marli.

She grinned. "This is what I do, love." She winked and pushed the door open.

Beyond the door, she blinked, adjusting to the dimmer lighting as she strolled in toward the librarian's counter. She glanced over at it. Not seeing anything notable, she continued on, making a show of perusing the shelves as she went.

Marli followed the shelves toward the back of the library where the office appeared to be. Another glance confirmed it was empty, with several stacks of un-processed books on the returns table. The arch next to the office door opened to a spiral staircase leading down.

She eased down the metal steps on silent feet, scan-ning the level as she descended. This room was even dimmer than the last, though it was lit.

Is the light always on?

It smells different down here.

Stale, but free of the male funk. And eerily silent, un-like the rest of the mountain that was full of the sounds of the tribe that lived within it, along with the machinery that modernized it. There was only the slightest buzz of electricity feeding the low lighting.

With a quick glance down each of the rows of shelves, Marli moved on down to the next level, repeating her actions. The stairs ended at the third level, which was also lit.

Drawing a deep breath, the space smelled of ancient books and documents with the slightest of earthy tinges. The scent of male dragon was undetectable here. What was detectable was the scent of female dragon—but not completely dragon. The dragon scent had a different flavor than anything Marli had scented before.

The fine hairs on her nape rose. She wiggled her tingling fingers, claws ready to extend in a blink.

Light illuminated the rear walls and ceiling of the back corner.

Sticking to an outer wall, she crept her way around the perimeter of the archive, ears strained for any sound, eyes sharp for movement.

Breath held, she eased forward to peer around the edge of the last bank of shelves.

She didn't know what she was expecting, but it certainly wasn't what she saw.

Shirtless, the librarian stood by a work bench loaded with vials, grinding equipment, bottles of liquids and a bowl of dragon detritus.

A female?

What the fuck is going on?

She appeared to be scrubbing her hands with the shirt she'd been wearing in the elevator. Her breasts were bare.

Marli watched as she withdrew another shirt from a nearby satchel and pulled it over her head. Next she placed a bound book on the table, grabbed a pen from its surface and began writing with quick, urgent movements.

Marli's brain sped through twists and turns to comprehend what she witnessed. What this meant.

A female, hidden among the males.

They both froze at the sound of Eamerson's voice. "Hello?"

"Damnation." The librarian muttered, tapped the pen on the table for a moment, finally slamming the book closed, the pen atop it.

Marli ducked back into the shadows as the librarian spun around, drew a breath, eyes closed as though to calm herself. The peaks of her breasts reduced into her chest so that her shirt lay flat. Her jaw sharped, and shoulders widened. She winced when her hips narrowed. With a huff, the librarian opened his eyes and hurried toward the stairs.

Breath held, heart pounding, processing what she had just observed. They thought they had a shape shifter of some kind. She couldn't have imagined a kind such as this one. Not really.

Figure it out later, Marli.

As soon as his—her—footsteps sounded up the stairs, Marli lunged forward to peruse the workbench. Pulling her phone from her pocket, she snapped photos of everything. Flipping the book open, she hesitated. "Dragonsdammit!" she hissed between her teeth.

An experiment ledger! Dates, identities, goals.

Should I take it? No, that would tip her off.

Instead, she snapped pictures of the ledger's entries, working backward several pages, then jumped all the way to the front to work forward. Setting it aside, she investigated the rest of the room, which was full of supplies for a librarian to do their normal job.

Just as a voice echoed down from the upper level, Marli noticed a heavy wooden door at the back of the room. A quick try of the handle confirmed it was locked. The lock itself looked similar to that set in the closet's mirrored wall, made of brass instead of gold.

Not having seen the tunnel doors for herself, she took pictures and made a mental note to ask Sten about them.

"The archival box I'm looking for should be in the earliest section," Eamerson explained.

"And you think it's down here?" the librarian sounded sceptical.

"I stored it down here myself," Eamerson didn't hide his annoyance at the challenge. "A correspondence series in aisle three, bay five."

"You could have just told me that and waited upstairs."

"Why shouldn't I come down here for myself? The archives belong to the tribe."

The librarian huffed and cleared his throat. His footfalls were a little heavier on the stone floor as he led Eamerson to the directed section of the archive.

Marli eased forward from the storeroom door. When the librarian's back was turned, she exposed her location to Eamerson.

At his nod, she darted down the nearest dark aisle on silent feet toward the stairs. Easing up the steps, she peered over the tops of the tall shelves to confirm that Eamerson kept the librarian occupied so that his back was to Marli's escape.

As soon as she reached the library's main door, she slipped out and pressed her back to the wall, staring at Sten.

"The deputies didn't find anything else on this floor... Marli? What happened?"

"This is so... complicated. The librarian is..." she sucked in a breath, trying to find the words, wide eyed.

"Is what?" Sten hissed.

"Complicated."

"Huh?"

"The imposter, yes, but it's..."

"Complicated."

Marli nodded, handing Sten her phone so that he could see the photos.

He growled as he swiped through. "I'd say that's complicated."

"There's more."

Sten's brows went up, prompting her to continue. "She... is a dragon... but not quite a dragon—I don't think."

"She?" Sten rubbed a thumb against his temple, closed his eyes, and shook his head.

"Yeah."

They were silent until Eamerson emerged from the library with a cartload of boxes from the archive.

Noting their expressions, he said, "Council room?"

Sten nodded and hit the button for the elevator.

Chapter 24

Marli, Stenlen, Eamerson, Goliath, and several others stood inside the mountain's interior runway hangar, waiting to greet their king and report on mountain events in his absence.

Jori and Kymri returned in the small plane, escorting a few guests. The plane transported the royal couple, Elora, Jonathan, and another familiar face.

Marli smiled at GPSA Agent Carson Perenga as he emerged from the plane. She was surprised and delighted to see the water dragon shifter again, after the night Jori and Kymri were abducted from Black River. She glanced around for Carson's mate. "Lirikai isn't with you?"

"She's following a lead for another case we're working on in the north. I have to join her as soon as the funeral is done here."

"You're here as a Global Paranormal Security Agency representative?"

Carson nodded, hitching a pack on his shoulder. "At Jori's request. He insisted the agency have a presence here for this important event. My bosses agreed and thought I was a good choice."

A large shadow blocked the sunlight as Odson's massive dragon form glided in to land nearby. He shifted into his human form as Carson tossed a pack to him.

"There's more coming," Odson grunted, withdrawing his clothing from the pack.

Marli averted her gaze as he dressed, watching for who else had followed.

Her breath caught as a glittering mist swirled into the hangar and dissipated, leaving a tall, handsome, fully dressed man in its place.

"That's Bayn Long, an old buddy of mine." Carson said. "Air dragon shifter from the east, though he currently resides in Toronto."

"Why does he get to keep his clothes when he shifts?" Marli frowned.

Carson shrugged.

"Something to do with air magic," Odson grumbled.

"He can transport others with him too, but I opted for the plane," Carson winked at Marli.

"That's because Carson's a chicken shit when it comes to air magic. I can't believe you'd rather get into a human tin can than fly with me."

Before Carson could respond, three more dragons arrived; familiar ones, from Aeleftheria.

Giddiness filled Marli's heart, catching her breath.

A giggle escaped her as Kymri stepped up beside her, holding a leather satchel with Aeleftheria's insignia. "Jori wanted to ensure that Aeleftheria was well represented at the funeral. For obvious reasons, the queen couldn't be here."

"Looks like I missed everything." Marli whined.

Kymri nodded, squeezing Marli's hand. "We'll catch you up once everyone is here."

"I don't see your mother."

"Kolina had something important she needed to do after ensuring we were all safe. She promised she'd be back before the baby is born." Kymri handed the satchel to Red.

"Thanks for your warning, by the way." Red said to Marli, clothes in hand. She passed the satchel off to Zayli and Neliah.

"We were able to rally the troops just in time to save my cousin's ass and keep the males off the main island."

Marli sucked in a breath, looking at Kymri. "What the fuck happened? Why did you need saving...again? I should have been there with you."

Kymri scowled at Zayli.

Zayli shrugged and sauntered further into the hangar. "Sten."

Marli spun around at the tone of her voice.

"Zayli," Sten nodded, his expression less than welcoming.

"We should... catch up, later. It's been a long time."

Sten's gaze slid to Marli.

Zayli glanced over her shoulder, following Sten's line of sight. She huffed, with a knowing grin and a shake of her head.

Marli bristled, eyes narrowing on Sten.

Jori approached, sliding a hand across Kymri's shoulders. "Everyone's here. Let's catch up in the Council Room."

Eamerson had already arranged for refreshments. He waited for everyone to settle around the large, round oak table that one of the males had made at his request.

"Well, we just had a crazy couple of days. What's been going on here?" Jori directed his question at Eamerson, but also looked to Marli and Stenlen.

"Eamerson finished planning the funeral, I'm about healed up, we may have an idea who let Clive and Merwin out—but it's complicated—and the males are still testy and argumentative," Marli's gaze slid between Zayli's cocky expression and Sten's stony silence.

"Not 'an idea,' Boss." Goliath said, stepping away from the wall he leaned against behind Marli. His face turning a darker shade than his usual ruddy. "On who let Merwin and Clive out of their prison. We know." He darted a glance at Marli.

Jori spread his hands, inviting him to speak.

Goliath cleared his throat. "The librarian did it. That's where all the magic books are." He nodded and stepped back to his spot along the wall.

Brows up to his hairline, Jori looked to Stenlen for details.

Sten scratched his forehead with his thumb. "He wanted to help, so we shared our theory of the face thief."

"I've been talking to the guys and they agree we probably have a spell caster among us. It makes sense."

Zayli snorted from her side of the table.

Kymri glared at her cousin.

"Uhm," Jori searched for words.

"I'm inclined to agree," Eamerson said. "I read King Kargassa's memoirs too, checked back through some of the mountain's housing and employment records. And I also had a few discreet conversations with other males."

Goliath grunted. "I was discreet."

"What do we know about the librarian?" Elora asked, leaning forward to pour tea for those that wanted it.

"Not much, except that her name is Sam Egan." Eamerson said, swiping his tablet screen to consult a file.

"Her?" Elora put the teapot down with a clunk.

Marli nodded.

"No one ever sees him outside of the library except mealtimes in the mess hall or at gatherings," Goliath said. "No one even knows what floor he lives on."

Marli shuddered, recalling the way the librarian had looked at her when she visited the library. She'd thought it was because she was an outsider. Now, it felt like more than that. A personal Aeleftherian grudge? Somehow, she didn't think she would have set the prisoners free because she was buddies with them. Clive and Merwin didn't strike her as library enthusiasts...though to be fair, it hadn't occurred to her that Goliath would be.

Reading from his tablet, Eamerson said, "Sam Egan. Lives on Sten's floor. But the other interesting thing I found when I went back through these records is that she arrived around the same time as the mystery male that Kargassa mentions in his autobiography."

"The one with Consortium connections?" Odson looked up from his phone.

Eamerson nodded. "Were you able to meet your contact on the subject?"

"Yeah, she's following up on what I told her, along with screen shots of the pages from the book."

"What's a Consortium?" Zayli asked, leaning forward in her seat, looking from Odson to Kymri.

"An ancient secret organization with very self-serving goals." Carson said. "The GPSA has been tracking them for a long time. They're difficult to flush out, and nearly impossible to shut down."

Odson huffed. "Seems all shit storms lead back to the Consortium in one way or another."

"So what is their aim?" Zayli pressed.

"They're shit disturbers," Odson sipped from his cup. "The kind that like to poke weak spots, in order to benefit from the chaos that erupts."

Bayn stood up, walking toward the windows. "And they came here to chat with Kargassa?"

"According to his book, they were interested in partnering with him. They wanted some artifact in his vault." Jori said. "He sent them away empty-handed."

"Not entirely, if they have someone here." Carson said. "I read Odson's screen shots too. The Consortium doesn't make casual acquaintances. If their liaison is still here, then they've had a solid feeler feeding them information all this time."

"Surely Kargassa saw that?" Marli said.

"He did," Elora said. "I thought about this while we were gone. Despite his colossal ego, he was also paranoid and careful. He kept track of people and events."

"I didn't find any such records among his files," Eamerson said.

"They wouldn't be. He kept certain things in his personal vaults hidden around the mountain. There are two in his bedroom." Elora said to Jori. Pain flickered in her eyes before her politician's mask settled in.

He swallowed with a nod. "I think it's time to start trying to pick some vault locks and see what he's been sitting on. In the meantime, we need to get this funeral over with and bury Kargassa for good."

"Two? Two vaults in the bedroom?" Marli leaned forward. "We only found one potential door."

Elora nodded.

"What do you want to do about the librarian?" Sten placed his empty cup on the table.

"When she was interviewed along with everyone else, she didn't say anything relevant." Eamerson jumped in. "There's more to report, but for now, she doesn't seem to know we're on to her."

Jori thought for a moment. "We'll just keep anything we know to ourselves for now and stay watchful." He glanced at Kymri's tired face. "Let's take a break so everyone can rest up before getting back to work."

Eamerson and Sten led Carson and Bayn out of the Council room to show them to their guest quarters, while the Aeleftherians gathered around Kymri and Elora.

Marli approached Odson, who still sat alone at the table, frowning at his phone. "What the hell happened while you were gone?" Marli demanded, sitting next to him.

He glanced at her, finished thumbing his message, then set his phone aside with a sigh as he studied her face.

She gulped. "That bad, huh?"

"I was in a meeting with my contact about the Consortium when my phone started pinging from Kolina Steelscale."

Marli nodded. "Kymri told me her mother was looking for her after Clive and Merwin attacked the island again."

"Right, well, she was waiting for me at Black River, demanding to be taken here so she could escort Kymri back to Aeleftheria."

"But Jori didn't want the location shared just yet." Marli clenched her jaw.

Odson nodded. "And apparently the comms tower was out of commission, so he wasn't getting my messages, which made it frigging hard to keep Kolina calm until we got the go ahead. Meanwhile, we started tracking Merwin and Clive's activities down the Continental east coast as they recruited."

Marli's heart hammered harder as she balled her hands into fists on her lap. "Zayli said Kymri ran into some trouble. She can't shift while pregnant."

"Even though Elora's negotiation skills are commendable, and she managed to persuade some of their recruits not to engage, the battle was fierce from the coast to the edge of the Aeleftherian archipelago. The queen intervened."

"Fuck. She didn't!" Marli gaped. "She left the citadel?"

"And the Council weren't happy about it either."

"No, they wouldn't be." Marli rubbed her hands over her face and back through her hair. "Fuck. I should have been there, Odson."

He gave her a sympathetic look. "I heard what happened."

She dipped her head, looking away. "I'm alright."

"Good."

"Clive and Merwin?"

Odson chuckled, "Those two knuckleheads are no match for Queen Regina. She forced them to ensnare themselves in their own devices, like the ones Kargassa used on Elora and Kymri. They aren't ever likely to get out of them either. At Jori's request, Regina gave them to Carson for the GPSA to deal with."

Marli's brows shot up. "Wow, really? Wow. She didn't let the Council execute them. That's... unexpected."

"And things didn't go over well on that front either. Regina has her hands full."

"That's a lot to take in," she slumped.

"I'm sure Kymri will tell you more later, but in the end, the good that came out of this is significant. Significant problems too, but some movement in the right direction."

"The council didn't go after Jori."

"Regina forbade it, after he acted to defend her realm and showed neutral initiative by having the GPSA involved. It was hard for the Council to keep screaming for his head as their primary enemy. And I tell you, they were loud, even with those massive oak doors closed."

"Oh, I know all about how loud they can be." Marli had been subjected to more than one reprimand in her career.

Marli glanced around, noting that they were alone. She stood to go.

As Odson did likewise, she noticed several fresh cuts on his neck and hands. She caught his large hand, pushing the sleeve up to see one nasty wound that went the length of his arm. She looked up. "Thank you for defending us, Odson. You're a good friend." She swallowed.

He shrugged, expression solemn. "I do what I can. What's right."

She released his hand and wrapped her arms around his waist, squeezing him hard.

He grunted, returning the hug. "We'll figure out how to make peace between these two tribes one way or another. This rift has gone on for far too long."

Chapter 25

Sten, Marli, Kymri, and Eamerson crowded around Elora and Jori, staring at the mirrored wall inside the master bedroom suite. Odson lounged on the white sofa, disinterested in participating in whatever revelations lay in the close confines of the closet.

They'd met early that morning to give a full report on their findings while all of their guests remained in their rooms.

At the mention of Marli's investigation into the librarian's workroom, Odson and Elora had exchanged grim looks.

"Yes, this is one of the vaults," Elora nodded toward the mirrored wall. "The other is in the bathroom."

"We don't have the key," Eamerson said.

"You won't need it for the other vault," Elora said, squeezing between Sten and Eamerson.

Everyone followed her out and into the cavernous bathroom.

"Behind the center mirror."

Three mirrors hung over the wide sink, supported by the same gold dragon headed brackets. None had keyholes in them.

Jori reached over and lifted the panel off of its brackets and handed it to Sten to set aside.

Affixed to the wall was an emblem with a dragon head set into a spiraling pattern, with five cylindrical holes.

"I saw Kargassa do this a few times. You need your claws, but don't allow the shift to make your human hand too big," Elora instructed. "Then insert your fingers into the holes. You may feel a pinch."

"And you think I can open this?"

Elora shrugged a delicate shoulder. "He was your sire. You have the same blood. It's worth a try."

Jori blew out a breath. "Okay. How do I do this?"

Elora explained how to do the partial shift.

Sten glanced at Marli as they waited. She hadn't spoken much to him since everyone's return—and the strained confrontation between himself and Zayli.

After the meeting, he had gone to talk to Marli, but she wouldn't answer his knock, though he was sure she'd gone to her room, nor had she answered his messages.

She still wouldn't look at him. Instead, she kept her attention on Jori and the vault.

He moved closer to where she stood, leaning against the wall, arms crossed.

"Marli—"

"Later."

He rubbed his temple with his thumb and turned away. "Right."

What was there to say? About Zayli?

Yeah, we fucked a few times when we ran into each other over the years...

"Okay, here goes…" Jori murmured, inserting his extended claws into the golden finger holes. "Ouch, son of a bitch, that's more than a pinch, Ma." He yanked his hand free of the lock, blood beaded on his fingertips, dripping into the sink.

Sten shoved thoughts of Zayli to the back of his mind. Marli was right.

Now isn't the time.

"Put your hand back and turn the mechanism. Hurry. Before it resets and you have to do it again."

He grumbled, but did as his mother told him to, with some hesitation, lest he be jabbed again.

The entire plate with the etched spiral and dragon head turned with soft clicks as Jori twisted his wrist. Finally, the mechanism popped. The entire piece came free, revealing a vault just large enough for several stacks of file folders and a few small boxes. Elora reached for the entire contents of the vault, cleaning it out completely. She handed everything to Kymri as she reached back inside, feeling the walls of the safe itself.

"It has to be here, I know it… Ha!" she said when there was an audible click. Extracting her hand, she revealed a gold key cradled in her palm.

Jori set the vault mechanism on the countertop as his mother took the lead back to the closet. "I have to do that again, don't I?"

Facing the mirrored wall, Elora slid the key into the lock. It clicked, allowing the entire panel to slide aside.

Jori sighed, seeing the second lock. "Guide me through this again."

"Partial shifts are tricky when you're first doing them. It doesn't take much to go too far," Sten said before he explained how to do it this time. "Focus on just the tips of your fingers."

"Not hard to do, since they're still throbbing. And bleeding."

Once Jori had control of his semi-shifted appendage, he lined it up to the lock, repeating the same process.

"So this means that any spells Kargassa had linked to himself can be accessed by Jori?" Marli asked, biting her lip.

Elora looked at her, considering her question, searching behind the concern she saw there. "I believe so. If you're worried about the collar and manacles Kargassa used to subdue us, Jori destroyed those."

"If there are more, I'll get rid of those too, Marli. They're barbaric." Jori grunted as the larger vault's lock bit into his fingers again, then opened.

"Holy shit," Sten murmured when the door slid aside to reveal the contents.

"It looks like Fort Knox in there," Jori breathed.

Kymri approached with the files cradled in her arms, the top one open. She glanced inside the vault and referring to the files, she said, "According to this, there are sixteen of those vaults hidden around the mountain. And two more larger ones off-site."

"What is it all for?" Jori stepped inside to examine the rows and rows of gold bars, stamped with Kargassa's symbol.

"A dragon's power is in their hoard." Elora said.

"So every dragon in this mountain has one of these?" Sten snorted, "Hell no."

"Everything of value that the males brought with them was given over," Eamerson said.

"So, he took everyone's shit, melted it down and claimed it. Nice." Jori grumbled. "Fucking disgusting."

"Aeleftheria has a similar system in that we collect precious metals and gemstones, but it's gathered and protected for the whole of the colony. The queen guards it, but she doesn't claim it as her own."

"Is that why he wanted Aeleftheria? To take their treasure?" Jori asked Elora.

"Probably, but he was also power-hungry. And enjoyed controlling everyone and everything around him."

"Did you know about this?" Sten asked Eamerson.

"On the surface, yes. I process all financials, but he kept all the details. I've never seen those files before." His eyes were glued to the folders in Kymri's arms.

"They seem to be all here. Each vault is inventoried. Hand written." Kymri shuffled through the papers. "That's mostly what these files are. The rest appear to be diary entries—for another book?" she gasped as she held up another sheaf of pages, flipping through them. "And profiles on everyone here, and maybe everyone he ever knew?"

"Am I in there?" Sten moved away from the shelves of gold toward the stacks of pages that Kymri held.

Flipping through the folder, she tugged one sheet out and handed it to Sten.

His fingers shook as he accepted it from her. He glanced up to see Marli watching him with concern.

Paper gripped between his hands, he left the closet and wandered out into the common area of the royal suite as he read the first few words. And the next.

Heart pounding, he left the suite.

Everything about me is right here.

Things that he'd never known about himself, Kargassa wrote in his own hand and hid away.

Leaning against the wall, he slid down to sit on the floor, arms resting on bent knees.

Marli emerged from the royal suite. "Sten? Are you all right?"

"He knew who my parents were."

"You didn't?" She sat next to him on the floor.

Sten shook his head. "I was left with a small dragon tribe in the mid-west. Not so different from the camp at Black River, really." His gaze dropped to the sheaf. "According to this, my father is on the west coast somewhere and my mother is Aeleftherian."

"May I see?"

Sten hesitated. "He analyzed me. Used my weaknesses to manipulate me. And I let him."

"To ensure your loyalty."

He nodded, swallowing the shame that rose from his gut and burned his heart. "I let him manipulate me because I saw him as a father-figure, even though I knew he wasn't and never would be." He'd allowed his awareness to slide right over all of Kargassa's faults, in exchange for his approval.

Marli's hand eased over his, pushing the paper away. She slid her fingers between his and pulled his hand against her chest.

"That's not who you are."

"Maybe I don't know who I am." He searched her face. "I thought I did. But I really don't."

"Of course you do. You just have a lot of noise drowning out your own voice. Your own thoughts." She was quiet a long moment. "Kargassa is dead. That past has died with him. Hasn't it?"

It had.

Sten's choice—the line he wouldn't cross—was that first signal to himself that enough was enough. And every day since then, he'd struggled against his act of disloyalty because he'd listened to his heart.

How can I make up for all the heartache I caused? How can I make things right?

He drew in a deep breath. "Marli, Zayli and I—"

"Shh. I don't want to hear it if it's in the past."

Sten blew out the breath he'd sucked in to make his confession. "It is."

"Then that's done too. She and I have a complicated relationship." She smiled. "Besides, after the claiming that went on in my bedroom, we're stuck with each other."

Sten chuckled.

"Sten, if you knew Zayli was Aeleftherian, why didn't you ever follow her back to the islands?"

"That would have been the smart thing to do." He shrugged. "I considered it. But, when I was off duty, I wasn't under orders to fulfill any missions. And I really just wanted to have a good time."

"How did you know she was Aeleftherian? We don't broadcast it."

Sten rubbed a thumb against his temple. "She, uh, has a tattoo on her hip."

Marli released Sten's hand. She rubbed her palms over face and back through her hair with a growl. "*Dragons-dammit*, Zayli." She sucked in a deep breath and released it. "That is going to have to be addressed. Though I don't think it matters much anymore. Thanks to Clive and Merwin's actions, we've got a whole bunch of folks that know exactly where Aeleftheria is now. But, that's a next week problem. Today, we have to prepare for a funeral and catch a shifty imposter who's still after some mystery object—which we have no clues about."

Jori poked his head out of the suite door, eyes bright. "Guys, we think we know what the librarian is after."

Sten laughed.

Marli threw up her arms, "Well, alright then!" She got to her feet and offered Sten a hand.

He accepted it and stood next to her, gaze fluttering over her smiling face. He pulled her into his arms and placed a kiss on the top of her head.

I love you.

He squeezed her closer to soothe the swelling in his heart.

She squeezed him back, burying her face in his shoulder.

Chapter 26

Marli led Stenlen back into the royal suite.

"Didn't take you guys long to make a mess of the place," she said, taking in the mass of papers spread across every available surface.

The boxes from the smaller bathroom vault rested on a side table along with several other objects, and the gold key that had opened the outer door to the larger vault.

"So," Jori turned with a hands-up, ready-to-explain gesture. "Get this—the key," he pointed to the gold key, "is the key to *The Key*!"

Marli shook her head, brows scrunched up, laughing at Jori's excitement. "What?"

"Another key?" Sten asked, looking to everyone else for a more coherent explanation.

Everyone else wore an expression of grim concern. Elora sat on the couch next to Odson with her face in her hands.

Jori looked like he was losing his mind.

"This is so wrecked! My mind is blown here, guys. Who'd have thought that not only would I discover that the myths and legends I was looking for in the middle of the Bermuda Triangle were real, and then—surprise—turns out I'm a dragon-guy." He held up his shaking index finger. "And not just any dragon-guy. The fucking dragon-guy-son of the king that was trying to conquer said mythological world and, and—get this—has the fucking power to wipe out all the dragon monarchs, and myself in the process. So yeah, I'm going back to the human world because none of this makes any fucking sense." He ran his hands through his long hair, disheveling it. "Or, I'm actually dead and rotting in my plane on that island where Kymri found me. That has to be it."

Marli's heart pounded in her chest as ice slid down her spine, processing what he said.

"What the hell does any of that mean?" Sten said to Eamerson.

Pale-faced, Eamerson said, "We figured out why Kargassa sent you after Jori instead of invading the island."

"He needed a proxy, in case the legend was true," Odson pointed at one of the mythology books.

Marli dropped onto the nearest chair. "The legend of the keys that safeguard the greatest dragon hoard known to dragonkind."

Kymri moved forward, hands extended. Across her shaking palms lay a gold seal etched with the same spiral background as the lock mechanism, but with two entwined figures instead of the single dragon head. A dragon encircling an androgynous human.

"I've seen that before," Marli glanced up at Kymri's strained face.

She nodded. "It's part of the central image of every Aeleftherian emblem on the island. We've been surrounded by it our whole lives, and I've never really paid any attention to it."

"They're depicted in the mythology books." Marli said.

"I've never read one," Sten said.

Marli explained, "The central emblem has three circles—or spirals—linked together. One has that image of the human and dragon. Another has a human engulfed in a flame, while the third has a dragon engulfed in a flame. I thought they were just cautionary tales."

"Of what? This key that you're talking about wipes us all out in a blaze of fire?" Sten asked, incredulous.

"Not exactly," Odson said.

"Yes, exactly that, for *some* of us," Jori said.

Odson leveled his gaze on his nephew. "That's not going to happen, because you're not going to attack the queen."

A nervous laugh escaped Jori. "Dude, she's bigger than me. She could fuck me up really bad."

Odson rolled his eyes.

Never having seen him do that before, Marli laughed, expelling some of the tension infusing her muscles.

"It's not funny, Marli," Kymri snapped.

"Yes, Kym, it is. Come on. Odson is right, we all know Jori has worked his ass off in these last months to ensure a peaceful friendship with Aeleftheria. And as lovely as you are, Jori, we also know that while you can fly, landing is practically impossible and you, therefore, will not be heading an invasion that would somehow result in you blowing yourself up. So let's back up here."

"I can land." He scowled. "Now."

"Since when?" Marli planted her hands on her hips.

"Kolina Steelscale taught him how, while we were away," Odson said.

"Huh, well that's great news," Marli gave Jori's shoulder a playful shove.

"Thanks," He smiled at that and seemed to relax several degrees, which eased the tension in the room for everyone else.

"Odson's been through the mythologies and he's spoken to his contact about the Consortium," Elora said. "Kargassa's notes are extensive, regarding them. They wanted to partner up to get the key that Queen Regina guards. The Consortium have the third key."

"That's where the myths seem to differ. One recounting says the three keys together open the greatest treasure known to dragonkind. One says they form a weapon, while another one says they open a gate of some kind. Kargassa's notes state that the keys were spelled, after the Great Divide, by a powerful being. This powerful being pops up in a few places at different times."

Jori continued, "This being spelled the keys so that each of the keepers could not kill each other to take the other's keys. They could only access and open the vault in friendship. Kargassa theorized that since I'm of his blood and by naming me heir to his throne that the key could make me accountable on his behalf. He really was going to use me as a weapon against Regina, and if the key triggered, then it would blow me up in his stead, hopefully taking out most of Aeleftheria, and her queen, along with me."

"Then he would just collect both keys in the aftermath and take control of the island and its treasure." Sten finished.

"And the Consortium?" Marli asked.

"Kargassa wouldn't leave that alone. He'd go after them too." Elora said.

"What about the imposter?"

"Kargassa's been keeping tabs on him—her—since the beginning. Even he didn't realize that she was female, though." Eamerson said. "He kept tabs on everyone in this mountain. Not just via the security cameras, but as soon as we had communications technology, he tapped into that."

Sten gaped. "I had no idea he was so paranoid."

Elora laughed. "No, you never witnessed his rants when it got the better of him. He was sure that you were bound to lead a rebellion against him at some point and usurp his rule," she said to Sten. To Eamerson, she said, "or that you'd figure out his real secrets and sell them to his enemies."

Eamerson and Sten both exchanged glances, looking deeply offended.

"That explains why he kept us so busy all the time." Eamerson said.

Marli asked, "So what more do Kargassa's papers tell us about the imposter? What can we use from that? How much of a threat is she to all of us?"

"We know she's after the Seal, for the Consortium." Elora said.

"Which we can't allow to happen," Odson jumped in.

"She obviously failed to open that vault in the closet, which means Jori truly is the only person that can open it. Therefore, just lock the Seal away for good."

"We need it for the funeral," Eamerson pointed out.

"Why?" Marli stood up to get a closer look at the seal that Kymri still held.

Elora sighed. "The burial chamber of the ancients is locked, to keep it protected. It's a sacred space and is part of our deepest heritage and our most ancient rites, back to the first known dragon shifters."

"That must be why we can feel the earth's magic more, the deeper into the mountain we go," Kymri said to Jori. "And why you can feel the magic in this key."

"Those that are closest to the royal blood lines feel it the strongest." Elora nodded.

Marli looked to Eamerson, "Does the tribe have any metal smiths that can make a duplicate?"

"There was one made already," he nodded toward the side table, where the small collections of boxes obscured the other 'seal'.

"Kargassa was prepared," Marli moved across the room and retrieved it to compare to the other. "How do we tell the difference between them?"

Kymri placed the original seal in Marli's palm. The real seal was lighter than the duplicate and it tingled in Marli's hand. She looked at Kymri. "Well, Commander Steelscale, we're going to need a plan."

"And there's not much time to form one before the funeral tomorrow."

"Odson and I are going to sort through all of Kargassa's papers and see if we locate where the communications transcripts for any new data over the last couple of months. There's bound to be more information here than what we skimmed just now."

"And we have to remember that the librarian has a key for the spelled doors to the tunnels—the mate to the one that opened the closet mirror. We don't know what else it opens."

Elora stood from the couch. "I'm going to wake our guests. We'll need to run through the funeral protocols with them."

"I'll go with you, Ma. Just give me a sec." Jori said.

"Glad you didn't totally lose your mind," Marli said to Jori. "But that was a lot dropped on you."

Jori snorted. "It certainly didn't feel too good knowing that my biological sperm donor abducted me to be weaponized—or as cannon fodder, whichever came first—against my mother's people."

"I'm glad it didn't go that way." Kymri slipped her arm around Jori's waist.

He bent to kiss her lips. "I'll be along in a moment. I need to speak to Sten."

Kymri smiled and joined Elora in the hall.

"I'll go—"

"Not yet," Jori stopped Marli from following Kymri. "I—Kymri and I are officially asking both of you to participate in the funeral ritual."

"Of course, whatever you need, sire." Sten said with a bow of his head.

Marli expected Jori to admonish him for the uncharacteristic formality, but the genuine respect in Sten's expression was clear.

Jori nodded and turned his attention to Marli.

"Of course, I would be honored," she smiled.

"Good, that's settled. We need food. I'm starving."

Chapter 27

Stenlen stood at his post in the great hall, watchful, until the proceedings began.

Kargassa's body lay in state on a carved stone slab, adorned with rich silks stitched with his family insignia. A titanium crown caught the torchlight.

He studied the grey face of his former king. A man whom he had followed for decades. Did everything he asked, and without question. Someone he viewed as a father figure—a replacement for the one he'd never known.

Stenlen would have been expected to participate in the ceremony as the head of royal security, though he'd argued he'd be better put to use doing his job to protect the current king from trouble.

But that was not what Jori wanted him to do.

His eyes swept the cavern that served as their gathering hall. The same hall where the tribe witnessed the unexpected and vicious change in leadership.

Jori had avoided this room.

Sten couldn't blame him.

The way Jori avoided the subject and hedged around the discussion on the event itself spoke volumes. He'd have to carry that, and figure out what to do with it.

The more Sten re-examined those events, the more sure he was about his own role. Events since then had solidified his decisions, and the sting of disloyalty faded.

As did Kargassa's conditioning and indoctrination.

With time, it was easier to see how warped his ideologies had been, and for his part, Sten recognized his acceptance of them as a form of revenge against past wounds and his need to belong, after years of drifting.

From the open door of the Council room, Sten had watched Marli and Odson in close conversation. It was clear they had a bond of mutual respect.

From his position in the Great Hall, he studied Odson, standing alone along the front row of males. Older than anyone knew. As old as Kargassa? Older? Battle-worn. Stoic. Always alone.

Mutual respect. Was that what Sten had hoped for with Kargassa? Someone to look out for him? An older male he could rely on and trust?

Sten swallowed hard, realizing that's what he wanted. Someone to have his back. Truly.

During excursions, he had relied on his wingmen—Clive and Merwin. They'd worked together a long, long time and he understood that they'd felt he betrayed them.

But for Sten, he'd always kept himself apart. He'd never trusted them, outside of their missions, because deep down he knew they viewed the world in a deeply different way than he did.

He just wanted that one person who would see him for who he really was. Someone that he could never reveal to anyone, as a mountain dragon. So he'd buried it.

Until Marli had walked into his life, challenging him with her sharp claws and glittering eyes.

She'd challenged his actions, his views, his way of life.

Without meaning to, she'd challenged him to unbury his heart.

His gaze found Marli as she entered the Hall and stood several paces to the side of the door. Concern swelled his heart as he observed her solemn expression.

Solemnity was expected at a funeral, even that of your greatest enemy, but he knew it was more than that. Jori told him what had happened while they were gone.

Aeleftheria had had another close call.

Marli hadn't been there to defend her home against the fleet of males that Clive and Merwin had recruited and led to Aeleftheria. They were vulnerable, and Sten was responsible for that. Who would come out of the shadows to attack them next?

Stenlen, Clive, and Merwin had been the original three to know the location of the island. Clive and Merwin's followers had been shipped away along with them, but no one could be sure some hadn't escaped.

He pulled his attention away from Marli to look upon the dead king's face again. He was responsible for that, too.

He swallowed the regret.

It was for the best, wasn't it?

He told himself that often. Maybe too often?

Elora entered the arch to the hall, her human husband next to her. She wore the same dress Kargassa had forced her to wear the night she was meant to witness her son's indoctrination to Kargassa's rule, as heir.

The difference was that her throat was bare of the magicked collar she'd worn since her capture and two decades of imprisonment in the mountain. A vibrant indigo flower was pinned to the fabric over her heart. With the three Aeleftherian warriors at her back, she entered the room with her head high, and with as much grace as a queen, gliding up the wide aisle between the standing males.

As Aeleftheria's ambassador, she represented Queen Regina.

She stood next to her brother. Odson looked down on her with a mixture of pride and compassion. He exchanged looks with Jonathan over Elora's head. Each of them took one of her hands in theirs.

Agent Carson Perenga and Bayn Long entered next, joining the other guests.

Eamerson entered ahead of Jori and Kymri. Marli fell in step beside him as they made their way toward the front of the hall. Marli caught Sten's gaze, holding it as she moved.

Low male voices rumbled up through the rows.

She'd been placed at Eamerson's side, not with the guests.

They stopped at Kargassa's feet, opposite Sten's position at Kargassa's head.

When Jori and Kymri entered the hall, Goliath, Craig, Pete, and a contingent of newly appointed deputies brought up the rear guard.

Stenlen swallowed. He should have been anywhere, other than where he stood. Looking down, he noted how his hands shook. He clenched them into fists and inhaled, slow and steady, through his nose. His heart galloped.

I shouldn't be here.

His gaze darted back to Kargassa's inert body, stretched out on the slab.

I shouldn't be here.

Not here.

His breath shuddered as he fought to control the tide of emotions suddenly washing over him. Sten blinked away the moisture threatening his vision and sucked in another steadying breath as Jori and Kymri took up their places at the head of the gathered crowd, facing Kargassa's outstretched body.

One more breath, as Sten worked through the steps of the ancient ritual he'd had to memorize.

The great oak doors at the mouth of the cavern closed.

The massive space fell eerily quiet as everyone waited in silence; solemn, respectful of the ancient rites.

The burial of a dragon king was a rare event.

Baritone horns filled the silence, shocking Sten's senses. The dirge rippled through him, disrupting the emotions trapped in his chest. The archaic sound called to their dragon souls, awakening the ancient seat of knowledge deep within them.

Sten's dragon expanded within him, stretching, making his dragon magic crackle as it met the vibration of the Dragon King's Dirge.

The horns fell silent. Sten drew a final breath, walking toward Eamerson and Marli.

Eamerson placed an open tome on Sten's upturned palms. Marli looped the chain bearing the image of Dragon and Human, the ancient symbol of unity, over his head and settled it on his shoulders. Her fingers lingered over his heart as she held his gaze for an extra second.

The apprehension in her face was replaced with compassion.

Her touch brought him peace, before he turned to Jori.

Stenlen froze as he met Jori's calm eyes. Eyes so similar to Kargassa's, it took him by surprise.

"Sten?" Jori whispered as the silence stretched.

"He's dead because of me."

"I'm alive because of you." Jori said without hesitation.

"As am I. And Elora." Kymri said.

Sten swallowed and nodded, dropping his eyes to the text.

One more breath. He looked up at all the waiting faces.

The mountain tribe.

Watching him, expressions solemn, waiting for him to speak the words they needed to hear.

The ancient dragon funerary ceremony, granting closure and a peaceful transition from one king to the next.

Looking at their faces, Sten realized they needed this as much as he did.

No matter the conflict, bickering, and confusion in the weeks since Kargassa's death, this moment was important to every male in this tribe.

He began the recital in a voice that carried across the hall, so that every one of Kargassa's subjects and guests would know he was being committed to the mountain's heart.

Sten's dragon enabled the ancient words to flow from his tongue, as though they were natural and familiar.

When he finished, he returned the book to Eamerson, who should have been presiding over this honor.

Not Sten.

Shoving the errant thought aside, he focused on the next task as he approached Kargassa one last time.

Leaning, he removed the titanium crown from his head with the tribe's insignia etched into its front. Fingers curling around its edges, he turned to Jori and placed it on his head. Next, Sten removed the chain from his shoulders and placed it on Jori's.

A collective exhale rippled through the gathered males.

Elora strode forward, unpinning the flower from her dress, and placed it in Jori's hand. "Queen Regina shares a bloom, bearing the seeds of Aeleftheria's sacred flower, as an offer of friendship between our nations."

Jori tipped the flower so that four tiny seeds fell out onto his palm. He dropped one back into the bloom, then stepped toward the stone slab displaying his sire's lifeless body. He placed the flower in Kargassa's folded hands.

Finally, he turned to the gathered. "We accept and honor this friendship. One seed shall be buried with the past, while the remainder will be nurtured with care." He placed the seeds in Kymri's left hand while he linked fingers with her right.

Goliath led the deputies forward. Together, the males lifted the slab, setting it on a shoulder each.

Stenlen led the way down toward the burial chambers. They stopped before another great oak door with the tribe's insignia carved into its face.

Jori moved forward, removed the crown from his head, and turned it so its circumference fit flush into the carved central piece. Next, he removed the talisman from around his neck and placed it in the carvings, where it nested within the circlet.

Elora approached, took his hand, and aligned it to the carving, whispering instructions on how to shift only his hand so that his claws were bared. Once they were, Jori spread his fingers to align with the holes and inserted them.

There was an audible click. He grunted, gingerly removing his claws from the holes. Blood dripped from his punctured fingertips. He spoke the ancient words, commanding the door to admit entry. Several more clicks reverberated within the wood, followed by the movement of gears. Finally, it released and eased open several inches.

Stenlen resumed the procession, spiraling downward until the mountain walls opened into another cavern, with walls and columns more intricately carved than anything he'd seen in the rest of the mountain. The walls were lined with bays of stone statues at rest, covered in centuries of dust.

So many.

Many were female. Not just kings. Queens too.

From before the divide?

Goliath led the males carrying the slab to the first empty bay and worked to slide it into place.

That done, they stepped back to give Jori access for the last step.

He focused on his dragon magic to transform his hand again, enough so that his scales were accessible. He broke one off and left it on the slab next to Kargassa as an offering.

Everyone that followed did the same, guests and tribesman alike.

Jori spoke the final words, asking the mountain to claim the king's remains so that he may rest.

A misty haze rose from the stone floor, rolled along the granite ceiling, and billowed from the surrounding bays, seeking the recent addition.

It slid over the colorful dragon scale offerings, absorbing their essence, reflecting the colors within the glittering, crackling cloud.

When it dimmed and receded back into the surrounding stone, the king's flesh and bone body had been replaced by a glittering stone replacement. Even the delicate Aeleftherian flower was perfectly replicated with its tiny seed nestled within its petals.

Stenlen's chest expanded with a deep breath.

It is done.

Chapter 28

Sam's body ached with tension.

I finally found it.

The procession had strolled right past the seal, currently imbedded in the great wooden door of the tomb.

After decades of waiting and searching and instigating, it was time.

Now or never.

Releasing Clive and Merwin from their cells hadn't provided the distraction needed to find and access the vaults. Failing that, Sam had been sure, *so* sure, she could get in using the gathered scales and blood Jori Mountainside had left scraped up the mountain face when he'd destroyed the communications tower.

The spells hadn't worked, just like they hadn't worked when she'd rarely managed to steal Kargassa's fallen scales. All she had was the stolen key to the warren of secret tunnels and the magic word. Her escape plan, succeed or fail.

She *needed* to succeed.

The Consortium was growing impatient. The time was approaching, and they wanted to be ready.

If she failed, she'd lose her sister for good, and any chance she had of being a Founder of the new phase.

She was valuable without the artifact, but the artifact was crucial to their plan. It was their key.

To what, she only had theories, since they hadn't confided in her. She wasn't a founder. Yet.

So, she relied on the spells their head wizard had taught her, worming her way through the mountain, watching and learning everything she could about every male that lived here.

She read every book in the archive and library. Even Kargassa's autobiography.

He'd thought he was smarter than Sam and the Consortium.

Kargassa had no idea how wrong he was.

His first mistake had been working with the wizard to create his imprisonment devices that he used on the Ambassador and others that had fallen prey to him over the years.

His second was in 'graciously', allowing Sam to remain in his mountain.

He'd had no idea when Sam simply walked in as one of his advisors, listened, learned and walked out again.

He'd had no idea how much Sam learned about him, his thought processes, his tribe, and his secrets.

Kargassa had dark habits that both fascinated and revolted Sam.

Some of which reminded her a little too much of the Consortium's menagerie overseer.

Thoughts of that monster tightened her body to near snapping as she waited her turn to make the offering at Kargassa's grave side.

What an interesting ritual.

So many scales left behind. How easy it would be to pluck and tuck a handful.

Better than scavenging the stinking aerie or various other sparring areas that the mountain dragons inhabited.

It would be easy to snatch a few to add to my dwindling collection.

Even though the plan was to get the artifact and escape, one never knew when they would need a contingency plan.

Sam glanced to the side, noting that Stenlen, despite his honored duties, watched each individual that approached Kargassa's corpse like a hawk.

As did the Aeleftherian.

Fucking Aeleftherians.

Hatred rose like rancid bile from Sam's gut.

Thieves. Their whorish queen sits on a treasure hoard greater than any in the world.

Sam didn't know what exactly the treasure was, just that it should be shared among all the dragons of the world. Even those, like herself, that were little more than just dragon shifters.

Selfish.

But once Sam had the seal that Kargassa had hidden, she could infiltrate the island and the Master would take this treasure back. Share it with all the world.

Sam suppressed the desire to sink a jagged claw into the Aeleftherian's heart as she passed her.

Stay focused. Get the seal, present it to the Consortium to share with the world, or whatever they wanted to do with it.

All she cared about was getting her sister out of the menagerie, then taking her own place among the Founders.

That's the deal.

Sam did her partial transformation, plucked a scale from the back of her hand, then reached out to place it on the pile of offerings.

Magic crackled around her hand as it passed over the scales like a magnet over iron filings.

She gasped, jerking her hand back.

Glancing between either observer, she clasped her hands together and solemnly made her way along the slow-moving throng.

The line snaked back toward the rear of the cavern.

Once the ceremony was complete, the new king led the procession out. The royal party stood next to the door as everyone filed out and back up the stairs, led by the deputies.

Sam lingered toward the back of the line, watching, easing aside to allow others to pass.

As the last dragon exited the tomb, King Mountainside closed and locked the door, sealing his sire in for eternity.

Shame. So much power in that sacred space. It belongs to everyone, and the king keeps it locked away.

Sam blinked, returning her thoughts to what was happening now as the new king disconnected first the emblem that was the key from the door, looping its chain over his head, and then removing the crown and replacing it on his head.

Done, he brought up the rear of the procession.

Sam resumed her place, casting glances over her shoulder as she plotted how to access that emblem.

The Seal. The Key.

Thrill rippled through her. After decades, it was *right* there. She mentally ran through the route to the closest tunnel access from her current position.

No, the best thing to do is return to the library.

At the first shadowy alcove, she ducked into it, using her ability to darken her hair and skin so that she would blend in.

Once the king passed her hidden position, she followed behind on silent feet, waiting for an opportunity.

He and his Aeleftherian dragoness exchanged low murmurs.

"I'm going up to rest while you're in the dining hall with your tribe," she said, reaching up to caress his cheek.

He caught her hand and kissed her palm. "*Our* tribe. You are my queen, and one day, maybe we can unite all the tribes again."

Ambitious. And not in the Consortium's best interest.

Sam's duties within the mountain had been to incite discord among the male dragons. Unity didn't work well for the Consortium. They needed their enemies fractured and distracted with rivalry. They'd succeeded in causing the Great Divide and had worked to ensure its continued success over the centuries.

A reunion of tribes could not happen—not yet. Not until the Consortium had all the seals, and sole control over what they guarded.

Then, if the tribes united, they would also be under the control of the Consortium, which was crucial for the next phase.

Sam remained behind them.

They finally reached the corridor beyond the Great Hall. The couple lingered, alone.

Sam held back in the nearest bank of shadows, listening.

The king removed the crown and the chain bearing the key. "Shall I bring those up to the council room?" the dragoness asked the king.

He nodded, handing them to her. "I'll ask Eamerson to collect them so they can be cleaned, and store them away later."

He bent and kissed her. They exchanged a few whispered words that Sam couldn't hear and parted ways.

The king joined his tribe in the dining hall, while his dragoness headed for the elevator.

Sam waited, fingering the vials she always kept on her person. She ensured that the king's Aeleftherian had entered the elevator, then confirmed she was still alone in the corridor.

Rifling through the vials, she found the correct one. Eamerson's tincture. More valuable than all the others, because he had more access than anyone else in this mountain, and his remnants were the hardest to obtain.

She could shift enough to pass as him at a distance, but Sam needed to be in close proximity and could not risk tipping her enemy off if the details were off.

She swallowed the vial's contents, controlling her gag reflex with a soft cough and a deep breath as she waited out the process. Each time was quicker than the last. Her body retained some memory of the shapes and colors required for the changes.

Done, her bones and muscles ached. Her skin itched and burned where it needed to stretch beyond her natural size.

With no time to waste, she accessed the elevator and made her way up.

Does the king know how valuable that key is? Does anyone in this mountain, now that Kargassa is dead?

The elevator door opened and Sam stepped out, effecting as much of Eamerson's stride as she could and made her way through the open council room doors.

The Aeleftherian consort looked up from a tablet set on the table and smiled. "I didn't think you'd be up here so soon, but I expect you're tired after all the work put into that ceremony. It went well, didn't it?"

Sam nodded, approaching the table. "It did." With the magic of the tincture, she had Eamerson's vocal chords, but not his style of speech. Normally should wouldn't talk at all so as not to give herself away, but she was in a hurry. "The seal?"

"Yes, of course. Right here," The dragoness moved toward a red velvet sac, tied with gold cord, with the seal set atop it. The crown lay on a blue sac, a third one next to it, which was black. The ritual book?

Sam swiveled her attention back to the key. The chain had been removed, and it gleamed under the sunlight streaming in through the tall windows.

"It is beautiful, isn't it?" the dragoness went on, running a fingertip over the central entwined figures. "Did you know we have a similar seal in Aeleftheria? Ours has a dragon encircling a water drop."

Sam grunted with a neutral head jerk and held out her hand. "Fascinating. Shall I?"

"Please. It's just a shame to store it away where no one will see it until the next king passes on, centuries from now." She sighed, slipping the seal into the velvet bag. Pulling the cord taut, she handed it to Sam. "Though best for its protection."

Sam gripped the bag in both hands, the sweat from her palms soaking into the fabric, and headed for the door.

"Eamerson?"

Sam froze and turned to look at the king's consort, brow raised as she'd seen Eamerson do on occasion.

"Take some time off. You're looking a little peaky."

Sam nodded and continued on.

Her heart pounded during the elevator ride down to the bottom floor. Sweat beaded in her hairline as she prayed there wasn't anyone waiting in the library for her.

Her heart nearly stopped when she stepped in and saw Goliath waiting at the librarian's counter.

Shouldn't he be in the dining hall with everyone else?

"Eamerson?"

"Gol—Frederick."

"I didn't see the librarian in the dining hall, and thought he'd like to join us."

Sam nodded. "I have to get a book from the archive. I'll see if he's down there." She rounded the counter and hurried down the steps, then kept going right down to the bottom floor.

Gather my things and escape now? Change, go back up and bide my time?

Her pulse ticked in her ears as the trembling in her hands increased.

She rushed into the back room, grabbed her rucksack from under the counter, and stuffed the velvet bag into it.

The need to flee was too great. She'd waited too long for this.

Her phone vibrated in her pocket, startling her.

"Damnation!" she grabbed it, reading the message.

"Damnation!"

Sam gasped.

So soon! And I'll be there to witness it!

Thrill rippled through her body.

The sound of footsteps descending the stairs jerked her from her excitement.

"Eamerson? Did you find the librarian?"

Sam grabbed her rucksack and frantically swiped the contents of her workbench into it. In her haste, a few vials fell to the stone floor.

"Damnation!"

Leaving the rest, she made her way to the door in the back corner, withdrew her stolen key, and spoke Kargassa's spelled words to release the lock.

Sparing one final glance at the space that had been her home for so long, regret crimped her gut.

Turning away, she let go of the door handle and hurried along the darkened tunnel.

Too focused on her next steps, Sam didn't notice the figure that slipped through the nearly closed door, placing the copy of Kargassa's biography in the gap as a doorstop.

In the weeks since Kargassa's demise, Sam had come to know these tunnels almost as well as she knew the library and archives itself. There were several exits to choose from that let out into hidden caves, wherein she would bide her time.

She'd already decided that simplicity was the best resource, and would follow the Aeleftherian delegation home.

Chapter 29

Marli adjusted her pack, waiting in the darkness, back some distance in the tunnel.

She'd dared to approach the edge of the cavern just once, and just enough to ascertain that it was a cave with an opening large enough for a human to fit through. A small human.

She couldn't get close enough to tell if she'd fit through it or not. She'd have to deal with that when the time came.

Wait and watch. Patience. Just follow the librarian to wherever she takes the seal.

Marli was used to waiting and watching. In a dark tunnel, buried under a mountain? Not so much. Half of her focus was devoted to keeping the cabin fever at bay as she listened to the librarian's movements in the cavern beyond. She was someone else that seemed to be accustomed to patience and waiting—according to what Marli had learned since Jori and Elora had read through all of Kargassa's notes, connecting the clues between the imposter, Kargassa's actions, and this new group.

Sam Egan. The librarian. Consortium agent.

Why haven't I heard of this group before? Aeleftheria had other enemies to keep at bay, not just Kargassa. Were they all connected?

None of her superiors had ever mentioned the group.

Would they have?

Marli chewed her lip. She'd always done her duty. Followed her orders. Gathered the information needed. Evaded whichever enemy was the focus of the mission.

Are the days of counting the mountain males as our top threat truly over?

Now, back at her job, doing what she knew best, her time in the upper layers of the mountain seemed surreal.

And yet, here you are, Marli.

She rubbed a hand over her marked shoulder, for the hundredth time since Sten had claimed her.

What the fuck are you going to do now?

She stifled the urge to sigh. Everything in the stone bowels of the mountain echoed too well.

Instead, she rubbed her palms over her face and through her hair.

You told him you wanted him, Marli. You also told him you couldn't stay.

Her heart slid up into her throat at the thought of parting from him.

She nearly laughed.

Your number one enemy. Stenlen Flintail. King's man. Well, I didn't rip his throat out, did I?

Does that count as failure? To fall in love with the enemy?

Love?

Yes.

She swallowed.

Can't think of that now.

Aeleftheria had a fragile truce with the Mountain tribe, with Jori at its head.

And what of these seals?

She wasn't sure she really understood it all.

W*hat is hidden in Aeleftherian territory that is so valuable?*

Were any of these myths real? Or was is all just a bunch of individuals believing in the stories and acting on them?

Doesn't matter, Marli. Real or not, your duty is to protect your queen and people from threats.

The threats are real.

The sound of rocks tumbling echoed down the tunnel, shaking Marli from her thoughts.

She crept forward, light on her feet to avoid making noise. Easing toward the edge of the tunnel exit, she blinked against the dim light filtering in through the hole that Sam climbed up to.

Marli watched as the librarian struggled to fit through the hole. Several rocks loosened but wouldn't dislodge.

The librarian muttered, "Damnation."

Marli could barely believe her eyes as she watched the librarian's body shift, shrinking and narrowing to almost a third of her size. She scrambled out and paused to regain her natural size.

"Well... fuck." She jogged out to the opening, dropped her pack and stripped down. Marli shifted into her dragon form, crouching for the cramped space, twisting around to use her claws to widen the hole, scraping some of the purple paint from her claws.

Dragonsdammit.

Returning to human form, she threw her clothes back on, grabbed her pack and went in pursuit of the librarian, keeping close to the dense pines nearby.

Seconds later, Marli heard the distinct sound of dragon wings flapping overhead.

In the far distance, three receding dark forms were visible.

The Aeleftherian contingent. In flight, the enemy dragon angled to follow them.

Shit.

"You're not seriously fucking considering going to Aeleftheria, are you?" Marli found a clearing, dropped her pack, texted Sten, undressed, and stuffed the clothing in the bag.

She shifted into her dragon again, hooked her pack with a purple claw, and took flight.

Sten paced the length of the windows in the council room, watching the distant group of Aeleftherians.

Elora had told them the gist of what they thought might happen with the librarian, and the Consortium.

Red had some pretty colorful language for that bit of information.

"And you just let the spy go?" Zayli snapped.

"Marli is on it," Sten growled, "and the imposter doesn't have the real seal."

Zayli huffed, but said no more.

"We should go," Neliah said. "The queen and council need to know about this new threat."

"I agree," Red said. "How do we get back to the hangar?"

"You can depart from the terrace," Jori said. "We're on standby to hear from Marli. We'll be in touch."

"Just remember the magical field around Aeleftheria inhibits modern communication." Red reminded him.

Jori nodded as he led them to the terrace in the adjacent room. "I remember."

The warriors shifted and took off.

Moments later, Sten squinted as an unfamiliar dragon appeared in the air, following the three Aeleftherians.

Who is that?

His phone buzzed.

A second lone dragon glided into view before climbing higher in the sky.

"Kymri, it looks like Marli is pursuing a dragon who is following the Aeleftherians."

Kymri rushed over to peer into the distance. "Yes, that's her."

He checked his phone. "She sent a message. It's on."

They exchanged glances.

"And who the hell is that?" Kymri frowned as a much larger dragon joined the trail.

Sten squinted as the unfamiliar figure approached from a different direction, following Marli. "Male. I've never seen that dragon before."

"Hey, has anyone seen Eamerson? He hasn't been around in a while and he was supposed to meet up with us after the funeral to discuss the next steps for the tribe." Jori said as he entered the room.

"He was here when the librarian come to collect the seal, posing as him, but left shortly after we secured the real one in the vault with the crown and the book." Kymri frowned. "He seemed a little preoccupied with some messages he received on his phone, and went rushing off."

"I wouldn't have thought there'd be any issues directly after the funeral," Jori turned his concerned gaze to Sten.

"I wouldn't think so either. Everyone would observe a period of respectful mourning. Any problems should wait until after that."

Sten pulled his phone from his pocket and dialed Goliath. "Frederick, do you know if any problems have popped up today that have required Eamerson's attention?"

"No, everyone's honoring the funeral rites. I don't think anyone would break that."

"No, I didn't think so either."

"I saw him headed for the hangar, though."

"When?"

"Ten minutes ago."

"Do you know where he was going?"

"He didn't say. Do you think there's trouble?"

"Yes, I think we should follow him in case there's trouble, but hang back far enough that he doesn't notice you. I'll meet you in the sky."

"Yes, sir."

Sten turned off the phone. "I have a bad feeling about this. Will you humor me and check the seal? We need to ensure we have the right one."

"Fuck. That's not good." Jori rushed toward the vault, going through the unlocking process much faster than previous times.

He went straight for the velvet bag that held the seal and pulled it free. "It doesn't have the chain loops."

"It's the duplicate?" Kymri asked.

Jori nodded.

Sten was already moving back toward the terrace.

"The only reason I can think of that he would switch them, allowing the librarian to escape with the real one, would be to take it for himself."

"And Marli is trailing her." Kymri rushed alongside them to the terrace. "I can't fucking shift anymore."

Elora put a hand on her shoulder. "Frederick is going out after them."

"How fast is he?" she demanded of Sten.

"Not as fast as I am." As soon as he reached the terrace, he stripped down.

Jori was pulling off his shirt, too.

Sten stopped him. "I strongly suggest you stay here. We don't know if he's working with anyone that could be looking for an opportunity to come after your family.

And I just sent Goliath and his deputies off mountain to pursue him."

"I can fly—"

"This isn't about that. If Eamerson isn't what we thought he was, then we have no idea what plans have been in effect all this time or what will happen next. I suggest you take your family down into the mountain. Maybe even those tunnels, now that you have the key to access them."

"We're not hiding," Kymri spat.

"Odson, Carson and Bayn are still here. They're spending time with the tribe down in the dining hall." Elora said.

"Good, go spend some time with them." Sten said before shifting into his dragon form and launching into the sky.

If he touches her, I'll rip him apart.

Chapter 30

Marli's eyes never left the librarian in flight, well ahead and somewhat below her. At this height, the only sounds were the winds howling around her head and back along her scales.

They'd just reached the coast and climbed into the upper atmosphere to avoid human eyes, when the scales on her nape prickled.

Glancing behind her, she saw only the sky, but from below a massive scaly form rushed up, colliding with her, stealing the breath from her lungs. Instinctively, she tucked her wings close to her body and spun away, with a hard kick to put distance between herself and her attacker.

Gasping, she managed enough distance to see that it was definitely a male she'd never encountered before, but smelled distinctly familiar. Someone she knew, but hadn't seen in his dragon. Her heart raced with fear and betrayal. Her mind kicked back to the attack at the waterfall and she nearly turned feral as she finally drew breath enough to snarl.

The urge to rend and tear overwhelmed her sense of cool tactics as she looped around him, raging and snapping.

He wasn't deterred as he lunged for her, jaws clamping on her tail. He snapped his head back and forth.

As she was wrenched from side to side, pain streaked up her spine so badly her gut churned, threatening to release its contents. Her pack slipped from her claws and disappeared into the ocean.

Using his force against him, she fought through the pain, twisting, and leveraged a hind claw into his face, slicing a nostril open.

He roared, releasing her.

She instantly tucked into a barrel roll, rocketing through the air away from him. It was all she could do to get her breath back and infuse her brain with enough oxygen to think straight.

She was sure the librarian was following her kinswomen back to Aeleftheria, but she couldn't let her get so far ahead that she lost her on the island.

The male dove after her again. Just as he was about to reach her, she spun away, snapped her wings open and changed direction.

A deep roar from above shook her to her bones.

No! Not another!

Frantic, she searched for the source so she could dodge the newcomer.

A male, nearly as big as Jori, soared toward her.

Her heart stopped.

Goliath?

Oh, goddess, no!

She rolled out of his way, belatedly seeing the other figures right behind him.

No, no, no!

Were they coming for her? For her Aeleftherian sisters? Aeleftheria herself?

Was this the end of the truce and the beginning of her home's destruction?

Her breath came too fast. She couldn't think; terror overwhelmed her as the first male arched toward her again.

She struggled to gain more altitude.

Another male soared past her so fast and hard, the turbulence nearly sent her into a tailspin.

She caught herself in time to see Stenlen collide with the unfamiliar male, forcing him down toward the ocean.

Gasping, she finally registered that Sten had just saved her.

Goliath and the deputies looked her over before following their leader to capture the offender.

Giddiness replaced the fear.

Marli swallowed a sob. She couldn't lose the librarian.

Sten caught up to her as her magic eased the pain in her spine, allowing her to increase her speed again. She still hurt, but no longer enough that it inhibited her ability to fly.

Gliding alongside her, Sten sniffed at her and huffed.

With his proximity, their magics mingled, increasing her regeneration two-fold.

She breathed a little easier, having him at her side.

Chapter 31

As they approached Aeleftheria Nisi, Marli was careful to ensure that they circled and landed together, so as not to alarm the guardians patrolling the skies around the archipelago. The nearest unit accompanied them to the landing tower.

It was already too late. The attack had cost her valuable time in catching up to the librarian, in order to intercept whomever she was going to meet, and she hadn't seen her land.

She shifted into her human form as soon as her claws touched the stone of the landing platform.

Goddess, it's good to be home again!

"You just got here. When did you leave again?" Launia, overseer of all guardians, ran out to meet her, snarling. "And where in the hells did he come from?"

"He's with me. We're here to stop an infiltrator." Marli ran toward the change room, grabbing random clothing to dress herself. With nothing appropriate for Stenlen, she tossed him one of the robes that were always kept on hand.

"Infiltrator? Wait? When?"

"They would have arrived right after Red, Zayli and Neliah."

"You're the only one that landed here after them. And here you are again."

"Me? You're sure?"

"Yes, Marli. I've known you your whole life... though..." Launia's gaze dropped to Marli's hands. "You didn't have any nail polish on your fingers."

"Shape shifter, probably spell work of some kind. Known name is Sam Egan, but we can't be sure it's her real name. I have to find out who she's meeting here."

"Hey, what's going on?" Red called as she ran over and grinned. "Bathrobe suites you, Sten, but it's a bit small."

"Red, the librarian is here and wearing my face."

"Fuck. Fuck! She followed us, didn't she?"

Marli nodded.

"This is real?" Launia asked Red. "A shape shifter?"

"Yes, alert the others without sounding the alarm. I'm going to warn my mother." Red said as she stripped down and ran off the edge of the launch tower, shifting in mid-air. Catching an air current, she arched toward the citadel's royal tower.

To Launia, Marli said, "I need to know where she—I—went so I can catch up to her without letting her know that we know she isn't me."

"Complicated, but okay. I'll spread the word among the other guardians. We can cover more ground." Launia considered Sten. "Sten? The one that attacked us?"

Sten held her gaze. "Yes, ma'am."

She turned her gaze to Marli, then back to Sten. "You caused a lot of damage that day. If you so much as squish a bug while you're here, I'll loose my guardians on you and there won't be enough of you left for anyone to know you were ever here."

"Yes, ma'am. Understood."

"Good. Marli, give him Delia's pants from the change room. She's tall. I think they'll fit." Her assessing gaze lingered a fraction too long.

Marli's lips quirked as she went back to grab the clothing, tossing it at Sten to wear under the robe. "Let's go."

Word spread like wildfire ahead of Marli. Guardians and citizens alike were whispering directions before she even reached them, sending her off on a winding path after herself. Sten trailed behind. On an island that was almost one hundred per cent female, he drew a lot of appreciative attention.

They'd ducked down a cobbled alley after the last woman had signaled to be quiet. Marli's target was near.

"Stay here," she ordered Sten, and slipped along the stone wall, crouching below the overhanging thatch. Beyond the cottage, the path opened to a grassy trail that lead toward the rocky beach below the cliffs.

Cliffs that house tunnel exits, much like the ones the mountain had. Only these tunnels were meant to be escape routes for the children and citizens when attacked.

She descended the stone steps, scanning the horizon. The fishing boats were all pulled in for the day, fish cleaned and set on racks to dry.

The beach curved around toward a bay from this point.

She nearly jumped out of her skin when Sten's shadow loomed over her as he descended the steps to the beach.

"I'm not leaving you alone again," he growled quietly, so that his voice wouldn't carry.

"You're going to give me away," she growled back.

He raised a brow. "Not unless she believes that I think she's you and I'm so lovesick that I couldn't let you leave me."

Marli rolled her eyes. "Be serious, Sten. Besides, from what I gathered when I overheard her on the phone, she's meeting someone here."

"There's an infiltrator here too?"

Marli nodded as his expression turned serious. "Who was that back there, Sten? Who did Goliath and the deputies take down?"

He swallowed hard, looking wounded. "Eamerson."

"Dragonsfuckinghell!" she breathed.

"That seal is the real one. It isn't the fake, Marli."

Marli's heart pounded in her ears. "Wh—why would he do that? This is bad. I really need to know who she's meeting. Fuck. Fuck! I'm so fucking fucked, Sten." She continued moving forward, whispering. "Find out what's going on in the mountain, take out any threat, get Kymri home safely. That was my mission. I failed every fucking part of it—Shh!" She ducked back against the cliff face, hand shooting out to press him back too.

She eased forward, daring a glance, straining for any stray words.

Fucking eerie. And why the hell didn't anyone tell me I needed a haircut? Though my ass looks great...

Marli's duplicate spoke to someone she couldn't see.

Sam's voice rose. "What do you mean he wants me to work here now? The Master promised that he would release my sister, and I'd be made a Founder once I brought him the seal."

Unable to hear the response, or see who Sam spoke to, Marli eased closer.

"I *hate* Aeleftheria—my mother is an Aeleftherian whore. You can't expect me to live here indefinitely. Decades in that mountain was bad enough, this will be even worse. Why did the Master change his mind and have it brought here?"

"Decades?" The unseen woman laughed. "I've been at this since the Great Divide. He changed his plan because I convinced him that I could safeguard both seals together, so that all he had to do was bring the third when the time was right."

"You're lying," Sam said. "He wouldn't risk that."

"You believed he would, long enough to bring it here, to me." The woman held out her hand, her face obscured by the deep hood of the plain cloak that draped her shoulders.

"This device is the key to my sister's freedom." Sam gripped her rucksack closer to her body.

"It's the key to many things far more important than your sister."

"Fuck you, old bitch," Sam swiped out with a clawed hand when the figure reached for her rucksack.

Marli waited, tense, to see who would win the scuffle. She couldn't let either of them get away with the seal, but she still couldn't identify the other woman.

Just let things play out a little longer...

"If we capture the librarian, maybe we can get her to tell us more about the Consortium." Sten whispered. "And where the third seal is."

Marli turned to look up at him. "Not without extreme force, if she has something to protect. Some of us would die before giving up information to the enemy. Besides, the seals were separated for a reason, weren't they?"

"We don't need to go after it, but knowing where it is and who has it is wise. Especially since the Consortium seemed to have known where the pieces were all this time."

"And Aeleftheria."

"Not necessarily. Depends on that player over there and what her true intentions are."

Sam cried out, stumbling back toward Marli's position, clutching the bag to her chest. She collapsed on the rocks, chest and arms bearing deep claw swipes. Blood soaked her clothes and dripped over the bag. She melted out of Marli's likeness to her own natural one.

The other woman lunged forward with clawed hands to grasp the satchel from her position, which brought Marli into her line of sight. She bore several bleeding claw slashes across her arms too. She turned and ran toward the ocean.

"Sten, alert the guardians and ensure they get Sam to the shamans at the infirmary before she bleeds to death." Marli ran after the cloaked figure.

The hood fell away from the woman's head, revealing light hair as she waded out into the water's rolling surf. The way the sun shone on her head made it difficult to discern if it was blond or gray. She dove into the water.

Shit.

Marli dove into the ocean after the woman and shifted into her dragon form to access her more acute senses. The islands were surrounded by an underwater landscape as complex as the one surrounding the mountain. It would be easy to lose someone there. The ocean floor surrounding Aeleftheria Nisi thrived as well as any tropical jungle, full of vegetation and fauna.

As Marli's eyes scanned the seascape, she swam forward, jaws open, tasting for any human or dragon scents.

The scent of a female dragon drifted over her tongue, inciting her to follow its trail to the source. Propelling forward, she approached the edge of the jagged land shelf, where the most vibrant ocean creatures lived. Beyond, the ocean dropped off into darkness.

Marli followed the trail as far down as she could, further still, even after it dissipated. She stayed as long as her aching lungs would allow, still failed to find the dragoness. She surfaced and dove again, searching. When she surfaced again, guardians circled overhead. From her vantage point, Sten was still on the beach with the librarian. Some of the guardians had him at spear point.

Fuck.

They won't kill him.
One more dive.

She stayed under as long as she could, but the scent was long gone, with no clue as to where the dragoness had gone.

Marli joined the others on the beach.

The librarian was still alive, clutching at the seal.

Sten held his ground, despite the spears pointed at him.

"I lost her," Marli said to Red as she landed on the beach and shifted.

Several others joined them, handing robes to the dragonesses that needed them.

"Who?" Red pulled on a robe on as more guardians arrived.

Marli nodded toward the librarian. "She met with a dragoness here. And it sounded as though she was one of ours, but I couldn't identify her."

Red sucked in a breath. "Mother won't be pleased about that."

"No, I expect not." Marli rubbed her hands over her face. "Sten saved my life on the way here. Is he under arrest now?"

Red scowled at the guardians. "Put those away. Councilman Flintail is an ally."

The guardians exchanged glances, but obeyed.

Shamans rushed down the stone steps toward the beach.

Red approached the librarian, looking her up and down. "So you're the infiltrator. The shape shifter."

"A-Aeleftherian bitch," Sam spat, shivering as her blood seeped into the rocks below her.

Red snorted. "And?

"Consider your words carefully, Sam. And maybe we'll help you get your sister back."

Sam's eyes swung to Marli's face, but she remained silent.

Marli leaned over her. "Let's start with the seal. I can rip it from your arms. Or you can hand it over. I can send the shamans away. Or they can heal you so we can discuss your master and your sister."

"And who your contact was," Red added.

Sam's lips compressed in her pale face.

Don't be stupid and fucking die on us.

Sam looked up at Sten, reached into the rucksack to extract the velvet bag containing the seal, holding it up to him.

He nodded, accepting it.

Marli breathed a sigh of relief.

Red signaled for the Shamans to approach.

The guardians surrounded their prisoner as she was transported up through the village to the citadel.

Sten reached for Marli's hand. She linked her fingers through his, allowing him to pull her into his chest. She sighed as his arms enveloped her, his cheek resting on her head as he murmured. "I'm going to have to follow you everywhere just to keep you out of trouble, Marli. My heart can't take this."

She leaned back to look up into his face. Movement caught her eye on the low cliff top above them.

They looked to see Zayli watching them with a smirk on her face. She snorted, "You two are perfect for each other. Come on, the queen wants you in her council chambers." She strode away, leaving them alone on the beach.

Marli grinned up at Sten. "I know this really cool beach not so far away that you might like. Clothing optional—unnecessary, really. Great party crowd."

Sten chuckled. "Sounds a little hedonistic."

"It's a lot hedonistic. Interested?" She pressed her hips against his.

"Absolutely. But I desperately need to see you in the nearest library, soon."

She gasped, "Oh, I can help you with that, too. We have the best one in the world."

He lifted a brow, moving closer, eyes on her lips. "In the world, huh?"

She nodded. "Mhmm," She rose up to meet his lips, hips pressed to his. With a hand around his nape, she pulled him toward the cliff face, where the overhang would shield them from any witnesses.

Back pressed to the rock, she slid her hands into the open front of his robe and down into his borrowed pants.

Eyes alight with a roguish spark, Sten's hands pushed her own robe aside as he dipped to lick and nibble her breasts.

He was long and hard, and she was ready. "Now, Sten."

He obliged, nestling between her hot thighs, tip pressed to her entrance as he slid into her.

She sighed and smiled. "Mine."

"Yours," he agreed, claiming her mouth. "Always."

"Always," she gasped as he pumped faster. "Always." She moaned as she came, gripping him hard within her as he thrust several more times, finding his own release.

"Marli," he growled into her mouth as his tongue found hers as he surged into her.

Her arms encircled his wide shoulders, taking all of him, holding him closer to her heart than anyone she'd ever held before.

And knowing that this time, it *would* last.

Chapter 32

Black River

Brandt Homestead

Marli smiled up at Heidi as she set the coffee cup on the table in front of her. "You're still my favorite hero."

Heidi returned the smile as she took her seat next to Odson. "Elora, it's so good to see you again after all this time—you too, Jonathan. And congratulations on the little one coming. You're going to love being grandparents." She reached across the table to squeeze Elora's hand. "Alright, I know this isn't strictly a social call, so catch me up. This is Stenlen, whom I've heard a lot about?"

Sten scratched his temple with his thumb, looking at Marli. "Yeah, I'm sure you have."

"And you're here in one piece, so that's also a good sign," Heidi winked at him.

Odson sipped his coffee. "Sten is a chief member of Jori's council. And as such, he and Marli are working on outreach together on behalf of both tribes."

"And what does that look like?" Heidi wrapped her hands around her cup.

"Well, we have a lot of bridges to build."

Odson grunted.

"Friendship," Elora said.

"Mhmm. Sounds like the dragons are looking for allies? That means trouble."

"For everyone," Odson said.

"We can go over the details tomorrow. For now we're all here as ambassadors. Now that things are stable at Katoa Koro, Jori wishes to offer it as a home to anyone that needs it."

"The camp and the drifters?" Heidi's brows went up. "That's wonderful, and—"

"Complicated. Yeah."

Heidi laughed. "An idealist. He's definitely your son. What's Katoa Koro?"

"We voted on a new name for our home," Sten said. "It means 'Whole Hearted'."

"Voted? He knows he's a king, right?"

"Yes, but not really," Elora laughed.

"Katoa Koro is an excellent name for a mountain dragon lair."

"They were a scale's breath away from naming it Dragon-Man-Cave," Odson lifted his cup, eyes twinkling.

Heidi threw back her head, laughing, "They weren't!"

They talked on into the night, catching Heidi up on all the news that Black River needed to know to protect themselves in the coming years, as dragon intrigue was bound to ripple out into the other communities. Now, more than ever, they needed to create a strong network of friendships, in the face of the Consortium's efforts to tear them apart.

Marli stood up from the table and smiled at Sten, holding out her hand. "Fresh air?"

She led him through the screen door and onto the porch.

"I never in my life would have thought that doing this kind of work would feel good."

Marli squeezed his fingers. "Hopeful?"

"Crazy, isn't it? We're still in conflict, but the focus has changed direction. And it feels more real than anything we've faced before."

"You're telling me? My superiors knew all about the Consortium and not once did any of them ever tell me that they were connected to any of my missions." She blew out a breath. "I'm glad we're working with the GPSA, too."

"I was surprised your queen allowed them to take Sam Egan into custody."

"She'd already worked out an agreement with Jori that some criminals were best given over to the GPSA."

Sten nodded. "Neutral judgment."

"Though when the Aeleftherian council figures out who betrayed us, that will be internal and vicious. Red is heading the investigation herself."

They stood watching the stars for a long time before Sten spoke again. "Jori asked my opinion about proposing to Kymri, to make it official."

Marli's heart flipped, and she smiled, "Did he? That's great!"

"You can't tell her!" Sten's eyes widened at her excitement.

Marli snorted. "I can keep secrets. Anyway, what did you say?"

Sten shrugged, "The worst she can say is no."

"What? You didn't!" she punched his shoulder.

"Ow! I did. I didn't know what else to say!"

"You don't have an opinion on marriage?"

"Not if I don't have any experience with it. I'd rather keep my mouth wisely shut." He pulled her into his arms, gaze fluttering over her features. "What is your opinion on marriage, Ms. Fleetwing?"

"If it feels good, do it." She grinned.

Sten snorted but couldn't resist laughing. "Everything about you feels good, Marli."

Her breath hitched, chest tight. "You feel good too, Stenlen Flintail." She reached up, stroking her fingertips over his lips and cheek. "Especially when you kiss me."

He bent his head, pressing his lips to hers. "Then I will always kiss you, Marli."

"Always?"

He nodded, his forehead against hers. "Always, if you'll have me." He drew a shaking breath. "I love you, Marli Fleetwing."

She grinned up into his beautiful gray eyes. Heart swelling in her chest, she leaned back to look up into his face, palms cupping his face. "I will have you for always, Stenlen Flintail."

DRAGON
BLOOD

Dragon Island Series

JODI KENDRICK

Next...

The very foundations of Aeleftheria Nisi are shaken when the royal heir is forced to choose between duty to her people and a destined lover that fate shoves in front of her.

Kymri & Jori

Marli & Stenlen

Astred & Kai

JodiKendrick.com

Want to know what happened when Jori and Kymri went after Clive and Merwin?
Read Dragon Steel – Kolina Steelscale's story.

(Dragon Steel is the first of a new spinoff series and is a complementary story as Dragon Island book #1.5. Its events are concurrent with Dragon Rogue.)

Dragon Steel

DRAGON STEEL
The world is changing and Kolina Steelscale must learn how to bend with it, or risk breaking her chance of a stronger future.

Read more paranormal romance check out ~
The Global Paranormal Security Agency series:
Awakened, book #1

The Global Paranormal Security Agency

Newsletter subscribers can download a free digital copy
of *Awakened* at JodiKendrick.com

Note to the Reader
Thank You!

Dear Reader,

Thank you so much for taking the time to read Dragon Rogue. If you enjoyed it, please consider leaving a review on your favourite platform.

Dragon Rogue follows Dragon Heat and is concurrent with Dragon Steel, where you find out what happened with villains Clive and Merwin after they escaped from the dungeon.

For free downloads, to join my newsletter and browse my growing library for more books with *Romance, Adventure and Passion*, visit **JodiKendrick.com**

-Jodi

Dragon Island

Dragon Heat
Dragon Rogue
Dragon Blood

EveL Worlds : FUCN'A

Tough Nut
Diamond in the Ruff
Honeyed Nut
Gorilla in the Hiss
FUCN'A Collection One
Pedigree Collection

Global Paranormal Security Agency

Awakened
Surfacing
Polestar
Aquatic Investigations
Prowler

Enchanted Ardor

Wish

Finely Aged

Dragon Steel

The Kindred Chronicles

Healer
Mercenary

The Nightshade Guild

Destined Time
Trial by Blood

The Soaring Dragon Chronicles

Return Flight
Changeling

About Jodi Kendrick

Jodi Kendrick lives in Eastern Ontario Canada with her *Favourite Person* and chompy furbaby, while their adult children explore the wider world.

As a romance author, she writes in paranormal, fantasy, steampunk & gaslamp subgenres, and sometimes delves into urban fantasy and paranormal women's fiction. Her characters are often quirky, sometimes cranky, but they all woman-up and get the job done while their partners ensure they survive with all their bits and bobs attached.

A history enthusiast and word dabbler most of her life, she enjoys exploring 'beyond-the-everyday' and the 'time-before-now', discovering relationship threads weaving individuals through time and place. She's rarely seen without flashy notebooks and colourful pens.

Follow Jodi on Social Media: